Scars of a Magician

by

Robert B. Herring Jr

Absolute Author
Publishing House

New Orleans, LA

Absolute Author
Publishing House

Scars of a Magician

This book is a work of fiction. Names, characters, places, and incidents, are products of the author's imagination or used fictitiously. Any resemblance to actual events or locales or persons living, or dead is entirely coincidental.

Editor: Dr. Melissa Caudle
Cover Design: Chocolatecitycomics
Author's Photograph: Robert B. Herring II

Library of Congress Cataloging-in-Publication Data

Herring Jr, Robert B

Scars of a Magician/Robert B Herring Jr

p. cm.

ISBN-13: 978-1-7337182-6-4
ISBN-10: 1-7337182-6-5

1. Fantasy Fiction 2. Science Fiction 3. Werewolves

Printed in the United States of America
0 1 2 3 4 5 6 7 8 9

DEDICATION

To my dad, my uncle and my grandparents. Because they molded me as the person who I am in so many ways from the good and bad, and I know they still live on throughout eternity.

ABOUT THIS BOOK

Derrick Blackwell, a teenage magician, fights his emotional demons on whether to walk a right path in life or dive headfirst into darkness. He lives in a magical hidden village in the Old Creek Mountains. While attending Seven Moon High School, Derrick comes across a mythic *Red Wizard Book* from a creepy old lady in the woods selling stuff from her carriage. Derrick thought he found just a cool magic book but realized what he had was a powerful wizard book that was supposed to be lost. After Derrick's last magic spell with the *Red Wizard Book*, he got caught with it in his possession by a few of his mom's patrol members. From that point, Derrick's choices would set off a domino effect that would change his life drastically.

Scars of a Magician

SAND BROOK WIZARD ACADEMY

TABLE OF CONTENTS

INTRODUCTION

In the New World existed a village called Seven Moon, nestled deep in the recess of the Old Creek Mountain miles away from the nearest town wedged in the old way of living. Farming, carpentry, fishing, and blacksmiths provided the mainstays of the daily grind for its citizens. Cloaked by strong magic from four ancient wizard kings who placed their magic inside a crystal at the top of Sand Brook Wizard Academy, from a casual perspective, Seven Moon appeared like a forest. The cloak kept outsiders from gaining the magical secrets and treasures allowing the wizards, witches, magicians, ogres, elves, gnomes and fairies to mingle and exist without being mocked or bothered from outsiders. Ruled by the Royal Family who lived in Sand Brook Wizard Academy; the village brought growth while different cloaked magic academies and others sprouted within its boundaries.

Seven Moon's patrol members who wore black and gray uniforms and badges to indicate their rank guarded and protected the village from their enemies which comprised witches, wizards, and a few mythical creatures.

Derrick Blackwell, a seventeen-year-old copper-skinned Aborigine magician who stood five-foot-eleven inches, with black locks, brown eyes, chestnut brown skin, and a slim body frame aggravated the guardsmen. Unfortunately for him, they didn't like him much because he caused trouble around the village.

Known for carrying his hoverboard along with his magic notepad which rested in his back pocket, he made a spectacle. As a kid, he adored his grandfather Jarvis' magic spells. He begged and pleaded with all his might for his Grandma, Sabrina, to show them to him. It took Derrick months until he convinced her. According to his grandma, his pride swelled when she informed him that as a child Derrick learned the spells faster than his Grandpa at the same age. A bond he held dearly throughout his life.

While in Seven Moon High School, Derrick wanted to fit in and he knew being smart wouldn't cut it. So, he kept his grades low and hung with the wrong crew knowing it was wrong.

Derrick's parents worked hard for little in return, but they lacked the supervision and teachings parents are known to provide. He spent most of the time in his developmental years with his grandma. All of five-foot-five, dark brown skin with tattoos on five percent of her body, braided long gray hair, and brown eyes, with a mole on her chin, she always carried two knives on both hips.

More like a mom to him than his mother, always told tales of his grandpa. Grandpa Jarvis disappeared years ago during the second Dark Moon Wars against wizards and dark werewolves. Derrick was a baby when that happened. Folks around the village had nothing but kind words to say about his grandpa, but no one could confirm if he were alive or dead. His passion for magic grew as he listened to her stories of how, brave, smart and stubborn his grandfather displayed. "Derrick you are just like him," she repeated those words to him almost daily which embedded them into his mind.

His grandma gave birth to Derrick's dad at a youthful age, and Grandpa Jarvis always wanted him to follow in his footsteps, but it never panned out that way. He pursued a career in medicine and potion following in his mother's footsteps. Both of his parents worked for Seven Moon High School. Kayla, his mom, led the school as principal, while his dad, Jacob, held the position of the science and potion teacher.

1. Awakening of a Young Magician

Monday morning came too fast for Derrick, and he had a tough time getting out of his bed. His pet cat, Atlas, stood on the edge of his bed asking him to get up. "Derrick it's time for you to get up for school." Atlas' bluish-gray fur matched the morning sky as did his light blue eyes. Both tails flicked the longer Derrick procrastinated.

"Atlas, I just wanted five more minutes of sleep before I have to be at school." He pushed Atlas off the bed, pulled the covers over his head, and went back to sleep. "Oh okay, I warned you last time about this Derrick." Atlas leaped back onto the bed jumping directly onto Derrick's head. Derrick bolted upward which made Atlas sail across the room landing on a pile of dirty clothes. He glanced at the clock. "Atlas, this is your fault. I only have forty-five minutes to get to school on time."

Derrick, jumped out of bed. He quickly tossed on a pair of pants that lay on the floor. He bolted over to his closet, grabbed a white dress shirt then his vest that hangs on a nearby chair with his school crest on it. "My brown boots, where are my boots?" He reached under his bed shoving Atlas's cape and his magical bo, utility belt before he snatched his brown boots. Quickly, he shoved his foot into one, and then as he hopped on one foot toward the door he slipped on the other. "Oh, I can't forget my notepad or my tie." Derrick left his bedroom followed by Atlas toward the kitchen. He took a few bites of blueberry pudding with his black tie in his left hand. "Now Derrick, don't eat too fast, let me help you with that tie of yours." She lifted her wand. "Tie tight, tie right, tie to my delight."

Atlas lay by the fireplace next to Sabrina's pet Static wolf Silver.

He grabbed a red apple and then headed to the front door. He snatched his hooded trench coat and scrambled to put it on.

He grabbed his book bag from the hook, threw it over his shoulder, and then retrieved his hoverboard.

He placed his apple into his mouth and opened the door. "See you later Derrick try to stay out of trouble, you hear me?" "Hmm." *That surely won't happen today.*

Derrick closed the door, walked down two steps and lay his hoverboard onto the ground, stepped upon it, pulled out his wand, and then aimed it at his hoverboard. *No time to waste.*

The hoverboard gradually lifted as Derrick bit into the juicy-delicious-red apple. *What will the dawn of the new day have in store for me today?* A broad-white-tooth grin flashed across his face as the apple juice dripped from his lower lip.

Derrick flew into the forest zipping pass the redwood, sweet gum, and spruce trees. As he approached the Shrub elks, red flying squirrels scampered away, and then a Common Nighthawk scattered when he whizzes past them.

After fifteen minutes of flying Derrick emerged next to a large water stream and followed it along the mountainside of the Old Creek Mountains eventually arriving at the Seven Moon Town village. He gazed below at the houses, stores, library. Centered, Derrick quickly recognized his high school as he jetted toward it, then landed his hover broad and stepped off. He waved as he levitated the hoverboard to within reach, snatched, and then placed it in his book bag. *Here goes another school day.*

He took a deep breath and proceeded to enter the halls of Seven Moon High School filled with students and a variety of magical creatures.

The school made from strong magical clay and stone used by the tree elves created a fantasy ambiance as the artwork forged by gnomes. Ironwood spread along the floor which he admired. He grew used to the jade green with gray paint throughout the school.

Derrick stood for a moment in front of a plaque which honored Alvin Crow, an old brown skin wizard with an eye for architectural who designed the school.

As Derrick walked through the halls of Seven Moon toward his homeroom class, one of his magical peers pointed his finger toward him.

"Hey Derrick, I didn't think you were going to make it on time. I guess I lost that bet."

"Seriously dude, my mom would kill me."

Eghort, an elongated tall Yeti, with brown fur on ninety percent of his body with black eyes bumped into Derrick. "Sorry, I didn't see you there."

"No problem, you probably dusted a little magic onto me. Gotta go."

He walked to his maple-wooden locker and retrieved his textbook. His eyes darted to the wooden classroom door. "Here we go. It's time for Mr. Squirrely's class."

Derrick strolled into Mr. Squirrely's class and took a seat at a desk in the middle row.

Mr. Squirrely a slender five-foot-five man from Ireland entered shortly after that and placed his bag onto the desk. He removed his black derby hat which revealed his red hair. He wiggled his red mustache as he removed his black coat which revealed his brown tweed suit. His finger lifted as his hat and coat flew to the coat rack and latched onto a hook.

"Good morning class." Mr. Squirrely's accent seemed odd to Derrick who never could clearly understand him.

Derrick cleared his throat. "Mr. Squirrely, do you like London better than New World?"

"I'm always going to love my homeland, but the hospitality here is comforting. Now, for our school's motto. A true magician will never reveal his magic; he'll never stop learning with every step he makes." He scanned the room as he checked off the attendance roll. "Did all of you do your take-home assignment? I can't wait to see your new card tricks."

Maxwell raised his hand. “I want to go first Mr. Squirrely.” He retrieved his deck of cards and then shuffled them in diverse ways. He faced Derrick. “Take a card.”

“Sure, I’ll play along.”

Maxwell faced another student, Ethan. “Take a card.”

Ethan showed his card to the rest of the class, then turn back toward Maxwell.

“Mr. Squirrely, it’s your turn. Pick a card.”

“So far Maxwell, this doesn’t seem like a new card trick. Where is your creativity?”

“Don’t worry; I got it.”

Maxwell closed his eyes. “Show your cards to the class.”

His assistants flashed the cards so everyone in the room could see them.

Maxwell covered his eyes with his hands. “Now I want you guys to remember who had what card, and then the three of you are to switch cards and place them into your back pocket. Derrick, let me know when you complete this part of the trick.”

The three swapped cards.

“We’re done.”

Maxwell opened his eyes and then placed the deck back inside the card box. He flicked it three times. “Card deck, reveal the three cards.” Slowly the five of hearts, king of diamonds and seven of spades rose and floated about the deck.

“Are these your cards?”

“No!” The response came from all three of participants.

The students erupted into laughter.

“Without looking at your card, check your back pocket and remove it.”

Derrick, Ethan, and Mr. Squirrely each removed a blank white card.

“Check your hand.”

They gazed at their palms and on each was the ink outline of their chosen card. The class cheered and gave hi-fives as Maxwell returned to his seat.

Mr. Squirrely nodded in approval. “Nicely done Maxwell. Derrick, you’re next.”

Derrick grabbed Mr. Squirrely's empty glass jar and showed it to the class. He held his deck of cards to his teacher. "Take a card and show it to the class and then place it face down beneath the open end of the glass jar."

After Mr. Squirrely did as instructed, Derrick covered the card and the jar with his handkerchief, He made a coin appear in his left hand, and spun it onto the table. After several spins, he slammed his hand over the coin and pulled his hand back revealing the ten of hearts card. "That's not all folks." He lifted the handkerchief which revealed the coin still spinning inside the jar. Derrick brimmed in delight because his trick worked as planned.

For the next two hours, magician after magician presented their card tricks displaying remarkable skill. Finally, the bell rang.

Derrick huffed. *Now magic algebra, science, foreign language, and native history.*

Derrick sat in the back of Miss Star's class for geography with the heat beating on him through the windows from the sun. He waited for lunch and Miss Roberts' Science class to start and end, but right now, it was Miss Star's class.

He drew on his notepad as he daydreamed about Reign Hungry whom he had a crush on since the second grade. As Derrick's daydream started getting good, the bell rang. He couldn't be late to another of Dr. Snail's classes.

Derrick grabbed his books from his locker and tossed them in his book bag. He hurried toward Dr. Snail's class. On the way there, he ran into Reign who stood at her locker at the edge of Dr. Snail's room.

Reign the daughter of Ox Hungry, a magic day and night trader and Nia Hungry, a seamstress witch for the Seven Moon Village and sister to Dusk, an eight-year-old little girl. She radiated beauty as she grasped her cumbersome books. Her black-rimmed glasses and her long brown hair which she curled into a bun gave her an awkward wizardry look. She dared to be different not caring about a popularity contest and always kept her nose into her books. She sighed, and a frown developed across her face.

Derrick took a deep breath and strode to Reign. "What's wrong?"

"I can't believe this. Me of all people, I forgot to study for the exam."

"I'm shocked this is one of the most important exams of the year. Why didn't you study?"

"Because I have a lot going on with my other classes, and I dozed off to sleep."

"Well, do you remember anything from the year?"

"Somewhat."

"I hope you remember something. I wish we had time for me to give you some tips, but if we don't get to class in the next minute, we'll be late." As they walked into the classroom, Dr. Snell had already used his magic to summons up a location for the exam; he chose the Grand William Penn Theater.

The Grand William Penn Theater was massive and magnificent decorated in red, brown and golden red, brown and gold. Expensive paintings adorned the walls. Other than Dr. Snell who stood center stage, the place appeared empty although it could properly seat at least two hundred people.

Before Dr. Snell made the audience appear in their seats, he took a deep breath. "Now student I want you to be on your best behavior today. I have some important wizards and witches of the best academies attendance the exams today and tomorrow. I don't want you to embarrass yourself as well as myself so impress and leave everything on the table to get accepted."

Dr. Snell closed the curtains looked at the students then turn his head back. *I hope these kids can do it.* "From big too small to all different cultures let the audience appeared."

Once he opened the curtains, the audience waited for the performances to begin. Dr. Snell's clothes had changed to a black suit and a white shirt ripples down the front, black bow tie, white gloves and to top it off a patent leather top hat. The crowd adjusted their seating arrangements and then waited for the performances.

The audience thunderously clapped as he took a bow then introduced himself. "I'm the Great Snellensky, I'm glad to see you have attended and that you're enthused to witness my amazing illusionists which I have been working with for several years now so I hope you enjoy!"

He told the students to take a seat in the audiences. "First up, coming to the stage for you a talented, smart and amazing student of my The Great Derrick Blackwell, give him a big applause!"

He took a bow. "Quiet!" He allowed the room to settle. Derrick made his way to the stage. He surveyed the crowd as his walked up the three stairs.

A lump of nerves clumped in Derrick's throat. "Are you serious? I have to be the first one picked to come up?"

Dr. Snell scowled at him. *If he would only focus and stop slacking off, he could be great.*

Derrick walked onto the stage and stood in front of the audience as they applauded. He gathered his courage as the applauded slowly faded into silence. His heart thrummed against his ribcage as his palms sweat. He licked his dry lips. "Thank you, everyone." For a brief moment, his hands trembled.

Barrett Bloodstone a light-skinned, five-foot and nine-inches teenage with an eye patch over his left eye glared toward Derrick. He had dark blonde hair and garments were tailored by some of the best designers. *He doesn't deserve to be here. He's a momma's boy.* Barrett belly-laughed at the sight of the garments worn by the assistant and Derrick's poorly performed magic trick. "He's only going to choke. I can't believe Derrick is going first. I have more talent in my left pinky than Derrick has in his whole body!"

"Mr. Bloodstone, don't interrupt my quiz, or I'll turn your face into something repugnant."

"I apologize, Dr. Snell, for interrupting your quiz."

Derrick smirked, and from nowhere a large empty box appeared out of smoke. He waved his hands over it as it lifted and turned so that the audience could see that it was empty.

As the box slowly fell back onto the stage, he nodded and smile. He closed the lid with a nod. With a slight of hand, his magic wand appeared. "Now for your pleasure, I present a one of a kind sight." Using his wand, he tapped twice onto the top of the box. The box magically lid swung open revealing an assistant who wore a mangled-dirty dress man riffed with holes. His face reddened. *I used the wrong spell. That's the ugliest outfit I've ever seen.*

The audience erupted into laughter. Barrett stood and sarcastically applauded. "It was horrible! I told you he was no good."

Dr. Snell approached Derrick. "Now, now, audience. We all make mistakes in our training. This is no way to treat a fellow magician. Derrick, did you study?"

"Afraid too much by these results." Sweat dripped down his face as the spotlight seemed to get hotter and brighter to Derrick. "I'll do another." This time a mangy tiger appeared. He had to keep performing; so, he pulled up his sleeve a little and glanced at the words on his arm as he reviewed his hidden cheat sheet for the correct magic words. He finally had the right magic words to say*. Right, I'll cut assistant in half and try to salvage this test. I can't do any worse*.

Derrick quickly pulled his notepad out from his back pocket and retrieved a drawing of a stream machine which silver metallic, sharp blades that would slice his assistant. Derrick ripped the page out, held it up to the audience and with a big flash a stream machine appeared right in front of him.

Dr. Snell nodded in approval.

Derrick pointed his finger toward the audience and moved it back and forth. "I need one assistant. Who will it be? I chose you young lady to please join me on stage?

The audience applauded as Reign made her way to the stage.

"What is your name, Miss?" "Reign Hungry"

"Thank you, Miss Hungry. First, please inspect the stream machine. Is it real and are the blades sharp?"

She touched the machine and gently slid her finger across the blade. "Ouch!" She pricked her finger. "Yes, very real and very sharp."

"Please, this way." He led her to the side of the machine. "Get in."

Reign looked at Derrick with a cautious demeanor. He assured her that everything would be okay, so she climbed in the machine with Derrick help.

Derrick shut the door and locked her into it. He made a pocket watch appear in his right hand then swing it. "Reign breathed in slowly and out. Michou, mocu, manga." She fell into a trance. The audience remained silent as he activated the stream machine. He sliced her in three pieces with the stream machine. Blood splattered, and with a blink of an eye, a sheet appeared over her body. *This plan better work; or, I'll fail this test.*

He moved to the box he used for his first trick motion for his assistant to bring over the tiger. "Come!" She walked in the box with the tiger. Derrick locked both his assistant and the mangy tiger in the box.

Derrick walked back to the stream machine and waved his wand over Reign. He pulled the sheet away, and she vanished. He returned to the box and tapped his wand three times onto the lid. Nothing happened. He held up one finger. "Wait, a minute." He opened the box, and Reign popped out flashing a huge grin. From the back of the room, his first assistant in the torn dress walked down the aisle with the mangy tiger.

The audience applauded louder than did in the beginning.

Dr. Snell nodded. "Derrick that was quite a comeback from the brink of disaster."

"Thank you, Sir. May I perform one more?" *That boosted my confidence.*

"Not today, your classmates need to perform theirs."

Derrick took a bow as his eyes darted toward the assistant and tiger and made them disappear. He lifted Reign's hand, and they bowed together before they walked off stage and joined the line on the right side of the stage.

Dr. Snell rubbed his chin. “Barrett time for you to come up.”

As Barrett gathered his belongings and made his way to the stage, Reign leaned close to Derrick’s ear. “You know his grandson is the villainous wizard Samuel Bloodstone right.” “No” “Samuel and King Damarco were good friends at one time, but certain situations split them.

“No I haven’t, but we never have gotten along since the first grade. Barrett is a snob. He lives in that giant old mansion at the end of the village with all the rich stuck up wizards and monsters in the village. I know his parents invented the hoverboard”

Barrett glowered at Derrick and flashed a wry grin as if like he knew something Derrick didn’t. “Now ladies and gentlemen, I’ll begin by showing you there is nothing up my sleeve.” Out of nowhere, his wand appeared.

Reign’s interest piqued. “That wand looks familiar to me. That’s not Barrett’s wand in his hand that’s his Grandfather’s wand. I remember reading about that in the library weeks ago.”

On stage Barrett’s two assistants magically appeared wearing mock black lingerie which was not revealing. He guided one of the ladies to a wooden coffin and helped her in and then chained her down. Barrett’s second assistant brought him two boxes filled with a bunch of rats and snakes. He poured each box’s contents into the wooden coffin. His chained assistant screamed; so, he put on the lid. His second assistant brought a lock and then walked to the side of the stage. Barrett locked the coffin and then summoned up a spell. “As the magic in within me rises, so shall this coffin.”

The coffin with the assistant in it levitated thirty feet into the air. The other assistant stood beneath it. Barrett waved his wand, and the coffin descended at high speed down and crashed on top of the assistant with such force it put a hole in the stage and kicked up a lot of dust. Boom! Boom! It sounded like a freight train colliding with a brick wall. After all the dust settled, both assistants appeared in the hole and stood in the spot where the coffin landed.

The whole audience gave him a standing ovation.

Derrick pursed his lips. “I thought it was great, but I don’t like the evil smile on Barrett’s face.”

Barrett and his assistants bowed, and then he made them disappear.

Dr. Snell nodded in approval. “We’ll take a fifteen-minute break to clean the stage. Those of you that don’t get to perform today will have the opportunity tomorrow. And, Derrick and Barrett, the academies will inform you tomorrow if you are accepted.”

Derrick glanced over to Reign. “I see your smiling.”

“I don’t think I’ll have to perform today.”

2. The Tricks of a Lost Soul

Charles, a Crescent Elf, stood in the classroom's door frame waiting impatiently for Derrick to join him for lunch. Although short in stature in his natural-self, his magical ability allowed him to morph into any size, any creature, or any human. In the last two years since his transfer to Seven Moon High School, he stayed to himself until he met Derrick. They eventually became best friends as they were kindred spirits and liked to get into the same trouble as Derrick.

"Hey, Derrick, are you ready to head to lunch?"

"Yeah, I'm ready."

Derrick's head turned as they passed a gang of trolls stuffing Mr. Bishop a half-goat janitor into the locker.

"Help, why are you treating me like these? I don't fit."

Derrick frowned at the trolls. "Mr. Bishop, that's what you get for snitching to my mom."

Derrick and Charles entered the dark and empty cafeteria. "I guess we're early. There are no signs of the lunch fairies."

"Yeah but I hope they come soon; my stomach is growling." "Charles looked at the new banner for last year School Mud Ball Championships along wall. "Nice, we worked hard for that one."

A blue and brown rug ran all the way to where his mom, the assistant principal, and faculty sat for lunch.

The lunch fairies appeared like a small beam of light, and the cafeteria started to come to life. The candles spontaneously lit and pans of food appeared on the side table. Gnomes, witches, elves, ogres, warrior cats and magicians strutted in their unique styles into the cafeteria.

Charles stood in line for the special of the day. For some reason, Charles loved the food Miss Toad prepared for the special of the day. Derrick checked his bag to see if his grandma remembered to pack him anything for lunch. "Thanks, grandma, for the chicken and wild boar sandwich, boiled duck egg, an apple and a jar of milk. He spread his items onto the table and prepared to take a bite of his sandwich when Charles dropped his tray of who knows what on the table and then devoured it.

Derrick's eyes widened. "Hey Charles, you piled up your plate today."

"Yup." Food spit along with Charles' words as food hung out of his mouth.

"What did Miss Toad choose for the special?"

"Well, the special of the day was two gophers, a purple rabble toad with a side of toenails."

"Man, when you eat that, I can barely look at it. It's gross. The odor from the Gophers and purple rabble toad is intense. I bet it could peel the paint off walls."

"Just quit complaining and eat."

"Hey Charles, I just thought up a clever idea."

"What?"

"After lunch, we can mess with the gym teacher."

"Okay, I'm in pulling a prank on Mr. Cash. What's the plan?"

"I find this book called Red Wizard Book."

Derrick searched around the lunchroom before he lifted the lid to his book bag.

"Where did you get it?" Charles demeanor changed as he witnessed the Red Wizard Book.

"I found it in a creepy old lady's carriage in the middle of the woods. It had a spell in there to detach a head from a body and make his other body parts move by themselves as well."

"Sounds cool."

"I think so too. Let's finish our lunch and head to the gym."

The bell rang, and everything reverted to an empty room. Derrick stood first. "It's time for Miss Roberts Class."

"You know I always skip hers."

"Not today, we gotta do our prank on the way. Then we can laugh about it during Miss Roberts' class."

"Okay, let's make this prank happen."

"It won't be that bad. Today class is outside of the library. We get to enjoy the sunshine and a cool breeze."

"Well, this should be a breeze."

Charles and Derrick headed toward the library. Just as planned, they approached the gym and, then peeked inside.

The cylinder gym with a retractable roof and bleachers ran along parts of the walls on both sides provide ample room for games and pep rallies. The cherry oak gym floor stretched throughout, and in the center, a bottomless pit with wooden pillars submerged partially in the ground.

Derrick snuck in behind the wooden bleachers as Charles stood at the door as the look-out for Derrick's mom or any patrol members.

Mr. Cash wobbled his head. "And children, the next day I went fishing."

Every student yawned in boredom.

"The fish were trout, but I turned them into a marlin."

Derrick retrieved the *Red Wizard Book* from his bag, and his wand appeared in his right hand. He pointed his wand toward Mr. Cash's neck. "With an eye toad and a scale of a snake, I command thee to fall apart."

Derrick's wand began to glow and then glowed bright purple. A beam shot from it straight toward Mr. Cash.

Mr. Cash's eyes rolled into the back of his head, as he gasped for air. "Now the Marlin wasn't just any old blue marlin." He froze in place for a second.

The students gazed at each other astonished.

"Now children, where was I?"

Charles whistled toward Derrick signaling that patrol members were heading toward the gym. *Man, if Derrick doesn't hurry up, I'm going to leave him to face Patrol Member Thirty.*

Charles started getting nervous by every step the patrol members took toward to gym. *Forget this; I'm gone Derrick on his own.*

As they reached the gym Patrol Member Sixty-Seven, notices a strange figure leaving the gym, so he disengaged from the group to investigate. Charles immediately headed down the hall turned the corner and hid in the bathroom. *I must morph into a mouse.*

"Charles is you in here. If I catch you, I'll see to it you're suspended. You hear me!" *That was close. I better scurry off to Miss Robert's class.*

Derrick flipped through the *Red Wizard Book*, looking for the right words to make him undetected by the patrol members.

Derrick found it, waved his wand over himself. "No trace oh, no trace, oh no, trace oh."

The patrol members marched into the gym. Patrol Member Thirty stood in front of Mr. Cash and snapped his fingers in front of his face. "Have you seen Derrick or Charles in the area making trouble?" He failed to notice what had just happened to the gym teacher.

Derrick stood motionless and held his breath not sure if his invisibility spell worked.

Mr. Cash's lower half detached and walked forward. His arms separated, and like an accordion sprung back.

Beads of sweat dripped from Derrick's brow. *Oh no, they're going to find me.*

Surprisingly, the patrol members didn't see what had just happened, but the class did. They conducted a search in the gym for Derrick and Charles. "They're not here. Move out."

When the patrol members reached the door, the office called over the intercom for Mr. Cash. His body moved toward the intercom lever, but his head remained in place. Horrified, Mr. Cash screamed.

The patrol members turned around. At that moment they realized something was fishy, and it wasn't Mr. Cash's marlin story he had told.

Derrick snuck toward the exit, and mid-way he tripped over a steel-tubing frame that supported the bleachers. His knee smashed into another steel-tube. "Ouch! Son of a gun." He quickly covered his mouth with his hand. *Oh, no.*

"Derrick! We know you're in here! Just give yourself up and save us the headache of looking for you."

Derrick pursed his lips as he froze in place. *I'm still invisible to them. If I leave now, they might still think I'm in the same location.*

Patrol Member Thirty summoned a spell; the bleacher disappeared, and Derrick reappeared.

Derrick forced a thin-lipped grin. I'm shocked. *How did they find me so fast?* He glanced at the laughing students laughing.

Patrol Member Sixty-five reattached Mr. Cash to his body parts while Patrol Member Thirty glared toward Derrick. "Derrick get over here now!"

Derrick snail-paced his way toward him.

"What is that in your hands?"

"My wand,"

"Don't play with me, Derrick."

"What are you doing with that book? You shouldn't even have it."

"But I do have it, and it's mine."

"Do you even know how dangerous this book is in the wrong hands? Where did you get it?"

"I found it; so, if you think I stole it, I didn't."

"Let's go talk to Principal Blackwell about this little mishap and this book of yours. Let's go." He took Derrick's wand and the *Red Wizard Book* and abruptly escorted him to the office. The rest of the patrol marched behind them.

They arrived at Principal Blackwell's office within five minutes and stood in the foyer. Patrol Member Sixty-five entered the office and returned with Derrick's mom.

Principal Blackwell's brows furrowed as she clenched her jaw; her eyes filled with fury. She took the *Red Wizard Book* from the Patrol Member Thirty's hand. "Everyone leave but Derrick." She inched closer to Derrick invading his space. "Get into my office now." She stormed into her office, and Derrick quickly followed.

I'm in big trouble now. Derrick's heart pounded in his chest as his throat closed.

His mother glowered toward him. “I'm extremely disappointed in you. You need to stop creating trouble around here and straighten up! I'm tired of dealing with your tomfoolery! What do you have to say for yourself, Derrick?” She threw the *Red Wizard Book* onto her oak desk.

“I don't know. I guess I'm screwing up!”

“That's all you can say for yourself? You're not a screwup. I know you're much smarter than this, Derrick! Now, where did you find this book?”

“I came across it in a creepy old lady's carriage. She was selling stuff from it in the woods. She wouldn't sell it to me; so, I took it from her when she turned her back. Can I still keep it?”

“No! This book is too powerful for you now, but you can have your wand back. Your dad will hear from me about this, mister. Now, head to Miss Roberts' class and don't let me hear you were in any more trouble today.”

Derrick grabbed his wand while staring at the *Red Wizard Book* and then peered at his mom. Frustration painted his face as he trudged toward the door.

“Derrick, one more thing. What did that old lady look like who you stole from, young man?”

“She was a pretty old lady with brown skin. She stood five-feet two-inches, I think, and she had green eyes. She wore a purple cape with a hoodie.”

“Did you remember anything else about the lady?”

“No, she had her entire face covered all but one eye. Come to think of it. She had a tattoo on the palm of her right hand.”

“Okay, you can leave now.”

He closed the door and proceeded bolted toward his next class.

Derrick arrived at Miss Roberts' class five minutes after the bell. The sky was fair, and the cauldrons already lit. Miss Roberts tapped her foot. “Derrick, glad you decided to join us. I hear you were a little delayed in the principal's office.”

The class erupted into laughter.

“Now please partner with Reign.”

"With pleasure Miss Roberts." A sense of relief captured his expression because he was not good at this type of magic for today's lesson. He moved to Reign. "Now I'm the one who is relieved."

She smiled at him. "I've got your back."

"Thanks, what's our project?"

"We have to create a rain cloud and shoot a thunderbolt from it. Let's go one step further by changing the color of the sky to gray."

"I don't know about that. I just want to pass this project. Be my guest. I'll let you take the lead."

This class went smoothly for Reign and Derrick. They got the work done with time to spare — Miss Roberts strode to them. "I see you two have finished. Please demonstrate your project to the class."

Derrick stood back. "Reign begin the chant."

"Sunshine, sunshine go away, we want a rainy day. If you dare to bring rain, it will be our gain."

A beam of light shot up toward the sky. The whole atmosphere changed to gray, rain clouds swept over and poured abundant rain.

Derrick leaned into Reign. "Where's the lightning bolt?"

"Let me think." Reign pondered the situation. "I forgot to chant the ingredients. I got distracted by Charles; he kept transforming into cute little animals."

"You may stop the rain. Who wants to go next?"

Derrick waved his wand, the rain stopped, and the sky turned blue.

"You two almost had an 'A.' However, you forgot the lightning bolt. I grant you a 'B' plus.

The rest of the class finished their projects, some with flying colors and some, not so much.

The bell rang.

Derrick grinned toward Reign. "I like having you as my partner."

"Thanks, me too."

Charles shaped like a hummingbird flittered in front of Reign's face. "You want to fly with me?"

"Quit it, Charles."

"Okay, have it your way." Charles morphed back into his normal self. "Derrick let's go, school over for today."

"You got the right. See ya Reign."

"See ya."

Derrick and Charles bolted into the school to get their belongings. Derrick unlocked his locker door, grabbed his trench coat, and put it on. He took a deep breath as he snatched his book bag and hoverboard. "Charles, look! Reign still has her nose deep in a witch chanting book. I wonder where she was going."

"Man, why don't you two go as out on a date? I see the way you look at her."

"No man, we're just friends."

"It seems like you want more than to be just friends, and you're too squeamish to make the first move."

"You're wrong about that."

"Are you sure about that Derrick?"

"Yeah, enough with this; let's go."

Charles and Derrick strolled out of the school.

Charles stopped and plopped down onto the steps. "Hey, what happened to you when you left the gym?"

"I almost got caught in the bathroom by some Patrol Member Sixty-Seven, but I morph into a mouse to escape and make it to class as you can see. Do you still have that book of yours?"

"No, my mom took it from me after I got caught using it in the gym. Now I'm in trouble when I get home."

"Hope you don't get grounded too hard. I'll talk to you later, Derrick."

They did their secret shake and went on their separate ways. Derrick placed his board onto the ground and jumped onto it. He aimed his wand at his hoverboard air-lifted in the direction toward his home. Charles morph into an eagle spread his wing and flapped and flapped until he soared in the cloud.

As he exited the town village, he preceded through the forest and up the Old Creek Mountain for ten minutes until he emerged above a spruce tree growing at the edge of the Old Creek Mountains. Derrick soared in the sky as the wind brushed his face. He glanced at the clouds as they changed to dark gray sending him flying lower.

Bang! Crash! Rumble! The lightning and thunder came from afar, and then rain poured. Because of the wetness, Derrick slid his hood over his head. It was hard for him to see for a while through the thick rain making it difficult for him to navigate to his Georgian Colonial three-story gray house with black shutters. It seemed to blend into the gray sky and clouds.

He landed his board and stepped off. Water dripped from his trench coat making a puddle on the front porch.

Derrick entered, hung up his trench coat, and then placed his board against the wall. The stone fireplace and lit candles created a warming orange glow. He sniffed the aromas which drifted from the kitchen. Sliver, Derrick's grandma's pet Static wolf lifted his dark gray ears. He stood and shook his dark gray with streaks on silver fur.

"Silver, it's good to see you."

Silver pranced to Derrick and rubbed his head beneath Derrick's hand. His nose nudged it again to get Derrick's attention.

"Okay, boy. I'll pet you."

Derrick's dad, Jacob, slender, highly intelligent, and his demeanor meant business strolled past him with a tube of potion in his right hand heading toward his lab. "Hey son, I heard what happened at school today, and I'm extremely disappointed in you. I know your mom, and I weren't around when you were younger; and aren't around much now, but this trouble that you've been getting into must stop. You think about what I just said, and I'll talk to you later. Oh yeah, and you're grounded."

Jacob entered his lab and closed the door. Derrick knew he wouldn't see him for the rest of the night; he usually lived in that lab. As Derrick approached the kitchen, his grandma leaned over a cauldron stirring its ingredients. "You know your dad had a point to what he said to you. You know I'm usually on your side, but you know you have to straighten up and fly straight, right?"

"I know I could do better."

"Your mom is working late today; so, it's just going to be us for dinner."

"I get it. It's common for this house; work came before family."

"Why don't you come over here and get some stew?"

"I'm not in the mood for that." He snatched an apple and headed to his room. On the way, Derrick knocked on his dad's lab door. "Dinner is ready." Derrick listened for a response that didn't come. All he heard was animal noises and his father's gruff swearing. Smoke suddenly escaped from under the door. "That's my dad." He shook his head and made his way to his attic bedroom.

3. Where Spies Meet and Clues Begin

Earlier that day after learning about Derrick's stealing the *Red Wizard Book*, Charles knew he must relay the information to his master. Charles soared in his eagle form for a while until he descended into the greenery below to finish the last half mile to his Master's lair. He eventually landed in a nearby tree. He surveyed the area to see if anyone followed. He took a deep breath. *Alrighty then, I wasn't followed*. He landed morphed back to a Crescent Elf.

He walked up to a cave where two hooded men guarded.
"Passcode"
"Midnight werewolf rides."

The creatures glowered toward him, then nodded in approval for Charles to enter.

He removed his wand which glowed to guide him through the cave. The stalactite and stalagmites grew on parts of the ceiling and ground. He avoided the bat dung and scurrying rodents as he traveled for a while through a few large tunnels and eventually arrived at a dead end. "No worries here." Charles waved his wand which revealed a door which led into a massive room. *I always love seeing this place.*

Lord Barrett Bloodstone sat in a vast chair next to his pet hawk; Eco perched on a stand near him at the end of the massive cave. Charles walked up and kneeled before his master. "Lord Bloodstone, Derrick doesn't have the *Red Wizard Book*. Mrs. Blackwell confiscated and locked it away in her office. Do you want me to retrieve it?"

"Not necessary to risk putting you in danger. I will use my spy to retrieve it." Lord Bloodstone grabbed a piece of paper, wrote down his plan, and then tied it to Eco's leg. He used his wand creating a swirling vibrant-blue-galaxy portal for Eco who took flight through it and disappeared; the vortex closed. He gazed toward Charles. "I will break Derrick's wand during the Mud Ball Competition tomorrow. I need you to persuade Derrick to get his wand fixed by Uriah."

"Uriah, Master?"

"No worries, it will be me under the mask."

"But Master, wouldn't Derrick figure out who you are, eventually?"

"This mystic mask can disguise my voice and appearance. Now go do your job!"

"Yes, Master."

"Take your mission with you and leave. Take care not to fail me."

Charles bowed and left.

Lord Bloodstone flashed a wry-villainous grin. He glared toward the creature and his pet dark werewolves. "Go forage for food and bring back recruits."

The dark werewolves leaped away. He strode to his black-water mirror that floated along the wall. "As I gaze upon myself darker than evil, Samuel Bloodstone share this space with me. I summon thee to appear and deliver unto me thy presence."

The black water swirled and soon turned choppy as a small typhoon emerged until Grandpa's Samuel image appeared in the mirror.

Barrett bowed to Lord Samuel. "My Lord, our plan is growing close to the end, and you will be freed soon to take your revenge on the Royal Family. The *Red Wizard Book* is in Kayla's possession."

"It better be Barrett! I'm tired of this despicable place. The infamous wizard Samuel Bloodstone well rise again and lay waste to those who oppose me. Why does she have that book instead of Derrick? I need both."

"I will have one of my spies retrieve the book, and another bring me, Derrick." A bead of sweat ran down the side of Barrett's face.

"Your Grandmother told me to trust that you would get this done. Don't fail me, Barrett."

"I wouldn't dare fail you, my Lord. I'll make sure it happens." He bowed again, and then Samuel's image faded from the mirror.

***

The clock above Kayla's desk read eight o'clock p.m. at Seven Moon High School as she prepared for a meeting with the Royal Council. She blew out the candles in her office and glanced toward the door to see if the three patrol members she appointed earlier remained. *I must be careful*. She strode to a bookshelf and retrieved a dictionary. The whole bookshelf shifted to one side exposing a dark hallway behind it. She used her wand to light her path until she came to a dead end and an enormous pit. "Mighty ground beneath my feet grant me the stairs I seek." She tapped one foot onto the ground as a long staircase rose from the pit in a flash.

Kayla descended the stairs which led to a secret room in the school. Kayla stood in the middle waiting for the Royal Council since she arrived first to the clandestine meeting.

One at a time the Royal Council's hologram images appeared. First Queen Gabriella wore an ancient diamond hawk feathers, rose quartz in the center with a golden rim crown and a royal purple and black gown.

King Damarco stood six -feet one-inch with brown skin, black hair, brown eyes and carrying an average frame. He sported a black beard with gray streaks throughout it, he had on elegant clothes, and a small crown made from gold and ancient diamonds hawk feathers, sodalite and a bloodstone placed in the center. Follow by King Osborn, King Nile, Queen Allura, and King Canon, who wore regal-crested robes and jeweled crowns on their heads. When all members took their position, Kayla started the meeting.

"Thank you for coming members of the Royal Council. We have a few agents tailing a few suspects under suspicion of helping Barrett bring back Samuel. Plus, I now have the *Red Wizard Book* in my safe to hold until you send Royal Patrol members to retrieve it."

Queen Gabriella. "Thank you, Kayla, for that update. We'll send a several Royal Patrol members tomorrow to retrieve it. Where did you find it?"

"My Queen, Derrick had it in his possession."

King Damarco cleared his throat. "Is Agent Two still monitoring Derrick?"

"Yes, she is. The Dark Society has yet to make a move toward him, but I have noticed a spike of villages getting raided by strangers."

"Well, I will send several Royal Patrol members out to guard those villages, and maybe we should add a few around your home, Kayla." King Osborn stroked his long curly beard.

Kayla's eyes narrowed. "No! I think Agent Two has Derrick taken care of, but I will inform you of any changes, my King."

King Damarco pursed his lips in disapproval. "Well, keep us informed of any problems. Kayla, is there anything else you need to inform this council?"

"Yes, I think that a Moonstone Witch was the reason Derrick got a hold of the *Red Wizard Book*."

King Nile lifted his brow. "Are you sure about this accusation?"

"I'm certain. Derrick described her tattoo."

"Find out for sure; we're not going forward with this until we know for sure." King Nile's tone implied anger.

"Yes, Sir!"

King Canon licked his lips. "One last thing, have you or any of the agents find the other three book yet?"

"No, Sir! As you know they have been lost for years. My lord, maybe this one can guide us to the rest. I will see if we have any new leads, sir."

Kayla nodded averting her eyes downward. When she glanced upward, the Royal Council image's vanished. She took an alternative path towards a wall on the east side of the building. When she reached a dead end, she pressed a stone on the wall. It formed a door which Kayla exited. Outside she whistled for her broom, which flew fast as it arrived. Kayla sat on it and took off toward home.

***

An hour and a half later, Eco arrived at Seven Moon High School and landed on the window sill. Mr. Bishop approached Eco, grabbed the message from his leg, and then read the words on the message. "Steal the *Red Wizard Book* from Mrs. Blackwell's office and then use it to steal the compass from King Damarco. Deliver both to Charles. He'll take everything from there."

Mr. Bishop sensed someone in the shadows, so he searched the area. He chuckled at a rat sniffing for food. Mr. Bishop grabbed his cart and then headed back to his room in the school to follow out his mission.

***

Meanwhile, Derrick lay on his bed petting Atlas. Downstairs the front door opened, then gradually closed squeaking the entire time. *Must be mom getting home from work.* He bolted down the stairs stopping at his mom's broom which leaned against the wall. *At least she is home, but where?*

Derrick strolled up the stairs toward his room stopping at his dad's lab. He knocked once, then twice onto the door and waited for his dad to answer.

Finally, Jacob peeked his head out. "Hey son, did you need something?"

"Have you seen mom?"

"No, I haven't. Maybe, she went to bed."

"Dad, can I come in and help with a project or two?"

"Sorry, I'm extremely busy with work tonight, but maybe another night."

"Okay, Dad." Derrick's smiled turned downward into a pouty frown.

Jacob closed the door and locked it tight.

Derrick strolled up the stairs into his parents' bedroom. Kayla sat on the edge of her bed removing her shoes as part of her routine to unwind from her work day.

"Hi, Mom."

"Did you talk to your dad?"

"Yeah, he grounded me for a couple of days."

"That may be all well and good, but I don't think that's enough punishment. Me and your Dad work so hard at the school and have an image to uphold. This can't happen again, Derrick. Do you hear me?"

"Yes, Ma'am."

"I'll talk to your dad again in the morning. Now go to your room young man. Finish your homework too."

Derrick left her room and shuffled into his own in the attic and went to bed. His eyes closed immediately as a dream filtered into his mind.

***

Grandpa Jarvis's pet, Sky, a medium-sized brown Hawk with specks of yellow throughout her feathers flew from the darkness; her wings whooshed as she approached. At first, she circled the room screeching, and then landed onto Derrick's Bed.

"Sky, what are you doing in my dream?"

"Derrick, it's your Grandpa Jarvis. I'm using Sky to communicate to you."

"Grandpa, is that you?"

"Yes, it is I. My time is short to talk with you."

"Wait, tell me something about myself if you're really my grandpa."

"You have a birthmark in the shape of a dragon behind your right ear. Plus, you have a stuffed teddy bear that you slept with when you were a baby. It was brown, had a missing eye, and it also has a gold coin in the belly. Is that enough to prove who I am, Derrick?"

"Okay, you got my attention, Grandpa."

Jarvis manipulated Derrick's dream to show him future events in a flash they stood in the center of the village. The dark sky lit by houses on fire which jetted flames as tall as an oak tree. Dark Werewolves pillaged the village sending screams of fear ringing throughout. Derrick's family lay dead on the ground.

"Dark forces are all around you. Be aware of who's around you. Never forget that."

"But Grandpa, what does this have to do with me?"

Jarvis left before he could answer Derrick's question.

***

Derrick bolted upright from his dream in a cold sweat. He looked around his room. *Was that a dream?* He pinched himself. *Yep, just a dream.*

Now in a battle to get back to sleep, he decided to retrieve to a bucket of water to wash his face. Derrick used his wand to guide himself through the pitch-black house. Once outside, he noticed the wet grass from the scattered rain shower that happened two hours ago. He looked up and saw stars and a few comets rocketed pass leaving silver and blue trails. The cobblestone path reached the water-well; so he proceeded to it and then peered inside. The full moon reflected on the dark water. To the right of his foot rested a lever and bucket. He cranked and cranked until the bucket entered the water. He waited as the bucket filled, then heaved it back up. He used his hands to cup water and splashed the fresh water onto his face which calmed his nerves.

On the way back to his room, noises from his dad's lab drifted through the hall. He looked around, rushed over to the door, and then pressed his ear to it. His curiosity got the best of him as he slid his hand down to the knob.

It's freaking locked. Derrick picked the lock; and as he looked throughout the room, he tried not to break any tubes of potion. As he entered the lab past the animal cages of Flying Lizards, Hairy Sand Armadillo, Stone Rat, and a Golden Pheasant they awoke. In the rear of the room, a big square object glowed beneath a sheet.

Derrick cautiously approached hoping whatever rested beneath the sheet proved to do no harm to him. He lifted the sheet and in shock almost fell over a chair. On the floor of the cage, a dark gray, five-foot-six werewolf with a missing left front arm lay in a trance. The plaque on the cage engraved with the words "M.S. Property" caught his attention.

"Wait! Have I heard about the M.S. Property before in one of my classes? What does this have to do with my dad?"

More objects covered by sheets splattered the room. *My dad must be experimenting with the werewolf.*

Derrick puzzled about all his needed answers, but who would have them? *I'm going to speak with Mrs. D-Walled tomorrow.* Derrick's eyes darted toward the door as footsteps headed toward the lab, so he lifted his wand. "Go sheet, do your thing." The white sheet lifted and covered the cage and the other stuff he uncovered during his snoop. He grabbed a bottle of invisible potion from a table filled with potions and then poured half of it over himself. He returned it back and then hid behind a box.

Footsteps walked right up to the door and stopped. A bright light pierced beneath the door. A dark figure entered and studied the area. Derrick peeped over the box. *It's Dad.* Relieved, Derrick stood after the potion took effect and slipped past him and out the door bolting for his room. He jumped into his bed and pulled the sheet over his body.

Within seconds, Jacob poked his head into Derrick's room. He smiled as he gazed upon his sleeping son. Then, he walked back down the stairs.

Derrick decided to call it a night and fell fast to sleep.

***

The next day Sabrina knocked onto Derrick's door. "Breakfast is ready sleepyhead."

It seemed like he had just closed his eyes. "Just five more minutes."

"Now Derrick or do you want a cold bucket of water?"

"I'm moving. I'm up." He rubbed the crust from his eyes and then wiped the drool from his face. He didn't want to leave his bed, but he managed to do so. He retrieved a nice shirt and a tie from his closet, grabbed his pants from the top of a big pile of dirty clothes, and then quickly dressed. *My black boots. Where are my boots?* He looked underneath his bed for his black boots, snatched them, and then eased his feet into them. On the way out the door, he grabbed his magic notebook from his nightstand and placed it into his back pocket and bolted. On the way downstairs to get his breakfast, Derrick paused at his dad's lab door. *I wish I could ask him about that werewolf, but he'd kill me and ground me more for snooping.*

When he arrived in the kitchen, Kayla studied her notes as she ate her breakfast, Jacob sipped his coffee while reading

The Goblet Gazette. Derrick sat at the table in front of his cold breakfast. *Why is dad giving me the beady eyes?*

"Hey mom, dad and grandma."

"Hi."

"Kayla, it says here in *The Goblet Gazette,* that Blue Creek Village was attacked and pillaged by a group of strangers last night." Jacob's eyes narrowed.

"That's weird." Sabrina glanced over Jacob's shoulders to glance at the paper.

"Yeah, this has been the third village this week." Jacob dismayed shook his head.

Kayla took a deep breath. "Derrick, your dad and I decided that you are not allowed to go on that trip today to the Honor Museum. Is that clear, mister?"

"Yes, crystal clear." Derrick sat quietly stewing in his chair.

"Derrick, were you in my lab last night?" Jacob's eyes fixated on his son.

"No, but I was up last night because of a dream, then went to the well. That's all."

"Okay, if you say so." Jacob's tone filled with skepticism grated Derrick's nerves. "Don't let me catch you in there without me, okay?"

"Okay, Dad."

Nervous, Derrick chewed his fingernails. *Did I leave anything in there?* He rushed to finish his breakfast. "I've got to leave a little early this morning to get to the library to research an assignment. Then off to detention."

"As your principal, I'd have to say I'm pleased; but as your mother, what's gotten into you."

"You and dad said I had to straighten up." Derrick strode over to the mirror and checked his appearance straightening his tie. As he walked out of the house, he grabbed his trench coat, book bag, and hoverboard.

It was five-thirty a.m., and fog covered the area. Derrick's mind surrounded by thoughts of last night intensified. *I must know what that thing is. Why is it in my dad's lab?* He hopped onto his hoverboard and flew toward school.

Back in the kitchen, Jacob threw his newspaper onto the table, and then swallowed the last bit of his coffee. “I swear, somebody was in my lab last night. I know Derrick is lying.”

Kayla rubbed her chin. “Why didn’t you confront him about it? And, how do you know?”

“I was heading to the kitchen last night when I noticed some light piercing underneath the door of my lab. I went over to investigate. When I opened the door to peek in, the light was gone, and my animals were awake.”

“Did you find any clue to say he was there?”

“No, but…”

“Well, okay then, let’s move on to something different.”

“Sabrina, how is it keeping an eye on Derrick? Have you noticed anything out of the ordinary?”

“It’s okay. He’s just hanging around Charles, and there’s been nothing out of the ordinary, yet. I had Patrol Member Four keeping an eye on him when I couldn’t.”

“Okay, keep us informed of anything new.”

“Like I wouldn’t.”

Kayla’s eyes narrowed. “Jacob, have you learned anything from the dark werewolf in your lab?”

“Yes, but I haven’t fully examined him, yet. Plus, I want to do extra tests on him before he turns back into a human. I will have all of this in my exam papers.”

“You do that.” Jacob walked returned to his lab because he didn’t have a class to teach until later that day.

Kayla grabbed her broom. “Another day at the school is calling me.”

“I understand.” Sabrina grabbed her broom.

“Let’s fly. Seven Moon High School awaits us.”

4. Accepted to Something New

As soon as Derrick got close to the town's village, the fog receded and he could see everything: school, stores, barns, and more houses. Seven Moon looked beautiful in the morning with the lanterns burning throughout. Derrick landed his hoverboard in front of the library and stepped off then placed it onto his book bag. The extensive library with brown bricks and narrow windows provided the resource tools needed for just about any magic.

Derrick walked up the three steps of the library and entered through the massive wooden doors. "Where is Mrs. D-Walled?" *It feels spooky in here when no one else is here.* He looked around for Mrs. D-Walled who stood five-feet tall, light-skinned with brown hair and three eyes. From the corner of his eye, he spotted her placing returned books back onto the shelves. He strode to her and tapped her onto her back startling her which caused her to almost slipped off the ladder but caught herself.

"Thanks, Derrick, for startling me! I didn't need to fall off this ladder."

"Oh, sorry for that."

"What did you need?"

"Do you have any reference material on the M.S. or M.S. Property?"

"Let me see. It means Moon Slayers. The Royal Council created them years ago to protect the secrets of Seven Moon and other villages. They are the ones who handle the dirty work behind the scenes, but that's all I know about them. They're the ones who protected Seven Moon during the Dark Wars. There is no more information to give."

"Are you sure about that?"

"Yes, now let me get back to my work."

Derrick glanced at the clock and noticed his class is to begin in ten minutes. So, he hurried off toward his first class of the day.

On the way, he stopped at his locker to place his book bag into it. As soon as Derrick closed it, he sprinted into his homeroom and took a seat in the back next to Charles. "Hey, Charles, how's it going, dude?"

"I'm good, but I'm ready to go home."

"Class didn't even start, yet and you're ready to go home?"

"Yep!"

Derrick laughed out loud.

When Mr. Jones entered the room, the students engaged in loud chatter and juvenile antics. He rested his butt onto the corner of his desk. "Listen up everyone. Time for roll call." He called out names from his roll sheet and waited for their response.

As homeroom began, a hooded individual in his late fifties and stood six feet tall, with medium brown skin, and white streaks throughout his hair appeared out of nowhere aided by a walking stick. The students froze like statues.

Derrick rose readying his wand for a fight.

"Hold on there, Derrick. I'm Merlin, and I'm not here for a fight. I'm here to offer you a chance to attended Sand Brook Wizard Academy! We think you'd be a great asset if you attended."

Derrick stared at him for a second or two. "I think I'd like to do that."

"Here is a gift from Sand Brook Wizard Academy to you, a pendant of a green moon." Merlin attached it to Derrick's shirt. "Be ready around five a.m. tomorrow and have your bags packed. A carriage will take you there." Merlin raised his walking stick, tapped it onto the ground and then vanished. Everything went back to normal as Derrick stood right in the middle of class.

The entire class laughed pointing at him.

Mr. Jones' eyes narrowed as he pursed his lips. "Derrick, why are you standing in the middle of my class? Have a seat."

Shortly after Derrick took a seat, the bell rang, and he was off to his second class of the day.

Charles went behind him. "Derrick, what happened in there?"

"If I told you, I'd have to kill you."

"Spill the beans."

"An old man in a hood appeared and offered me a spot at Sand Brook Wizard Academy."

"So, you're saying an old man in a hood appeared in the classroom and offered you a chance to attend Sand Brook Wizard Academy?"

"Yes, that is right. His name was Merlin. See, he gave me a gift. Yup, I start tomorrow."

"That's good for you, but what's going to happen to me?"

"Hmm, other academies might accept you. The school day isn't over, and you can still get in somewhere, or you could go for the open tryouts."

"I guess."

"You'll just have to show up for a few classes now instead of skipping most of them."

"Isn't that calling the kettle black? You did the same thing for a while until you destroyed too much stuff around the village and had Patrol Member Four follow you home and to all your classes."

"Yup, but I paid attention to some of my classes. I'm in now, and that's all that matters." Derrick tapped the new lapel pin.

"You don't have to brag about it."

The two continued to meander their way toward their next class, turned the corner and almost ran into Mr. Bishop walking down the hall not paying any attention as he talked to himself. He pushed his janitor cart down the hall and around the corner before Derrick could say anything.

Derrick out of breath made it to Mrs. Cat's room before the tardy bell rang. He noticed Reign watching him, so he gathered himself and plopped onto his seat.

Reign glanced toward Derrick. "Everyone is anxious for the field trip to the Honor Museum."

"My parents told me after the last mayhem that I couldn't go, but lucky for me, I took a few permission slips. He grabbed one from his book bag.

Derrick forged his mom's signature onto the permission slip. As he walked up front to hand Mrs. Cat his slip, she gave him an odd look as if like she didn't believe his mom would allow him to go on this trip after his last trouble. Mrs. Cat nodded, and Derrick headed to the carriage to get a good seat in the back. By the time he arrived at the transport, all the seats in the back completely filled. So, Derrick sat toward the middle next to Reign.

"I heard you got into Sand Brook Wizard Academy this morning."

"Wait, how did you find out so soon?"

"I overheard Charles tell Sam about you getting accepted there. He didn't get accepted yet, to anywhere."

Sam was an older student held back several times at Seven Moon High School and a friend of Charles and Derrick.

Derrick gazed at her lapel pin on Reign's uniform. "Well, look who's talking! You have a green moon pendant as well, so congrats to you too."

"Yeah, I've been training hard to get into Sand Brook. Your grandma has been a great mentor for me."

The carriage filled with the remainder of the students, and they were on their way to the Honor Museum.

5. What You See, Isn't What You Get

In the hall of the high school Mr. Bishop turned the corner and glanced around. *I can't be seen.* Once he felt that he was alone, he slipped out a rare map of the school. This map had two options - It could show hidden passageways, or it could allow viewers to follow the movement of people in the school.

"Show me the secret passageway to Mrs. Blackwell's office, her location and the location of any patrol members."

The map outlined the way to her office, which went through a wall near where Mr. Bishop stood. Once he located the entrance, he searched the map to once again, find the whereabouts of Mrs. Blackwell and her patrol members who stood outside her office.

Mr. Bishop reached into his pouch for his magical flute to open the passageway. After the wall slid open, he pushed his cart into the passage and waited for the door to close. Once the door closed, his map glowed, and he proceeded off toward his objective of retrieving the *Red Wizard Book*.

***

It was seven thirty in the morning, and Barrett just arrived up for school. His lackeys waited for him to arrive in his fancy royal burgundy with a beige trim carriage. The carriage raced down the cobblestone road with two big colts pulling it. It came to a screeching halt right in front of the school. One of his lackeys ran up to open his door while another watched him exit and then kneeled.

Barrett looked around while he exited the carriage. His lackey closed the door, and the carriage took off toward the forests.

The taller lackey handed Barrett his bag as he walked toward the school for his class.

Meanwhile, on the way to the teachers' lounge, Kayla decided to see if Derrick attended his detention since he couldn't go to the Honor Museum. *He better not of skipped.* She raced upstairs and down the hall to the third door.

Mr. Oliver sat behind his desk reading *The Goblet Gazette* with a cup of coffee, and his feet up resting on his desk. He spat his coffee all over his paper when he saw Kayla standing in front of him.

"Where is my son, Derrick, today? He should be here in detention waiting for his next class, not going on that trip to the Honor Museum."

"Derrick never reported here today as you can see. Mrs. Cat told me everybody had slips for the trip, even Derrick."

"What? I didn't give him a permission slip for that trip. He was not allowed to go as a punishment!" Kayla's frustration boiled over in her eyes as she stomped out of Mr. Oliver's room on her way to the teachers' lounge.

Meanwhile, in the carriage, Derrick watched as the road turned from cobblestones to grass. They traveled through the forest until they approached the Honor Museum a half an hour later. Derrick had never visited this place before.

His grandma told him about the wonders and history that the Honor Museum held. It didn't look like his Grandma said it would, but Mrs. Cat said the Honor Museum served as one of the battlegrounds in the past, and it almost didn't survive. So, to protect its secret, they moved it to a wood cabin surrounded by a ton of booby traps, unseen Royal Patrol members and dogs who guarded throughout the area.

This wood cabin was old and falling apart. An elderly couple who sat in rocking chairs out in front as the carriage pulled up. The students filed out of the carriage and waited for Mrs. Cat to approach the elderly couple. They shook hands using a secret handshake. Mrs. Cat handed the elderly couple a scroll.

The elderly woman rose. "Welcome to the Honor Museum. Keep your hands to yourself and touch nothing."

By his first impression, Derrick thought that the Honor Museum had to be the world's smallest museum; but when he entered, he realized that what you saw on the outside was not always what you got on the inside. "You really can't judge a book by its cover."

Reigns eyes widened. "You're not joking."

The walls painted tan seemed boring. A fancy tangerine colored carpet with brown trimming ran throughout. The museum had beautiful chandeliers, granite statues, and pictures of famous alumni, faculty and the Royal Families. The place was enormous with so much to see and not a lot of time. They walked down twenty flights of stairs and strolled up to a picture filled with cats hanging along a wall to the left.

A Scholar cat with silver fur, blue eyes, and two tails jumped from the picture and landed right in front of them. "My name is Nave, and I will be your guide while you're visiting the Honor Museum today. If you guys can follow me, we can get started on your tour."

Mrs. Cat's class followed Nave past a statue of an ogre with one eye. Derrick stared at it for a moment before he caught up to the rest of the classmates. Nave stopped at one of the exhibits which displayed a few items from the first magician, Jacob Philadelphia, and next to it several of his belongings as well.

He discussed information that the students knew and a lot that they didn't know. The tour took them all over the two-floored building and past a secured, secluded area in the Honor Museum guarded my Royal Patrol members.

Derrick stepped forward. "Nave what is in this room and can we visit it?"

"No, it is a forbidden room."

Derrick caught up with the group who now stood next to a picture of his grandpa. His grandpa's exhibit included his wand, glasses, and hat. Beneath the picture a plaque which read - "A great wizard, father, and son, who disappeared during the Dark Moon War. These were the only things left from him, and we will never forget what he did for us."

"Why didn't they tell us more about him or what happened?" Derrick lifted his brow. "Hey, Nave, why didn't they talk more about my grandpa under his picture?"

"What! This picture is of your grandpa? He was a great wizard. You must be talented and brave like him. How are your parents doing?"

"They're okay. Wait, what does this have to do with anything? What do you know about my grandpa and his whereabouts?"

"Jarvis was my friend, and we worked together in the field years ago. Let's continue this tour. We are almost done."

"Wait, Nave. You know more than you're willing to talk about, don't you?"

He ran around Nave and stood in front of him as the class stood watching the interactions. Nave tried to go around him, and then under him, but Derrick blocked off his path. He lifted Nave off the floor and shook him. "What do you know about my grandpa, you pesky cat?"

Suddenly, two Royal Patrol members bolted into the scene. "Put Nave Down!"

Derrick took a deep breath let go of his grasp of Nave.

A patrol member grabbed Derrick's arm and escorted him out of the Honor Museum to the carriage. He waited there for twenty minutes before Mrs. Cat approached him. "You just embarrassed yourself and the entire student body. I have no choice but to report this to your mother. Now get back into the carriage and don't move."

Derrick climbed into the carriage and headed to the back.

"Not anymore. Move upfront so I can keep an eye on you."

Reign boarded the carriage and plopped right next to him again which brought a cheery smile to his face.

"You know, that was disrespectful of you to do that to our host, but I could see where you were coming from."

"I just wanted some answers from Nave. Nobody will give me a clear answer about my parents or grandparents. I found a few clues, but I can't piece anything together yet."

"What exactly are you trying to piece together?"

"I've never felt like my parents are my real ones. I don't look like them at all."

"You kinda do."

"Last night I found a cage engraved with M.S. Property. And, as a baby, I had a stuffed teddy bear with the Royal Crest. My baby clothes had the same Royal Crest."

"I'm trying to figure this all out. I'll try to help you."

"Yeah, that would be cool if you could." Derrick hugged her, then backed off. They both blushed, then looked away out the windows.

The carriage filled with the remainder of the students and then proceeded to head towards home.

6. The First Chess Board Move

Elsewhere in the office of Mrs. Blackwell, Mr. Bishop rummaged a long time through the office looking for the *Red Wizard Book* while continually watching at the map to locate any patrol members and Mrs. Blackwell. *The last thing I need is to get caught in here.* Books, paperwork, and contents from the filing cabinets scattered the room. He tossed another book after he couldn't find the *Red Wizard Book*. "Come out, come out wherever you are." He waited to see if his spell worked.

His eyes darted toward the map. *"She's coming and so are two Royal Patrol members."*

Frustration, nervousness, and panic came over his face. At that moment, Mr. Bishop knew he must leave. He glanced carefully at the map again to locate any new chambers in the office, but nothing appeared. His time had ended. He grabbed his cart and left the office right before Mrs. Blackwell entered.

As Kayla approached her office, she ran into two Royal Patrol members. "We're Royal Guard Member Twelve and Six. The Royal Council sent us for the *Red Wizard Book*."

"How do I know whether you're impersonating a guard and not an actual Royal Guard member?"

They turned their palms upward. A Royal Crest glowed. "You're the real deal. No magic can do that. This way to my office."

When they reached it, her jaw dropped; her eyes widened. "Someone has trashed my office."

The two Royal Patrol Guards searched her office looking for clues while Kayla checked the secret room to make sure the *Red Wizard Book* remained.

She used her magic to slide the bookshelf to one side and then used an unlocking spell to reveal her secret room. "I'm relieved. The *Red Wizard Book* is still here. It's safe, but we still have a criminal on the loose. I'll have to put the school on lockdown." She handed the *Red Wizard Book* to the closest Royal Guard. "Here. Protect the book with your life. Take a few of my men to help if you need them."

"Okay, ma'am."

"The rest of you search this room for clues. He or she shouldn't have gotten too far."

When the carriage arrived back to the school, Patrol Member Forty ordered the students to stay in a nearby room.

Derrick glanced toward Reign. "Something is wrong. There are too many patrol members running around. They are searching for something."

"I agree. I wonder what's up."

Over the intercom, Kayla broadcasted an announcement to the arriving students. "Students of Seven Moon High School, please remain in your classroom. We are on lockdown protocol."

Derrick's eyes widened. "This is serious. My mom doesn't lock down the school for a simple drill."

As all the students filed in a nearby room.

Mrs. Cat exited the room to speak to Patrol Member Forty. Royal Patrol Guards Thirteen and Six bolted past Derrick and Reign. One carried a messenger bag with the Royal Crest. Four patrol members followed in close pursuit.

Sam bumped into Derrick. "What do you think is going on? She's your mom."

"I don't know, but I'm going to find out. Sam create a distraction so I can leave without detection. Reign, I need your cape."

The three nodded.

He tacked it to the wall and cut a line down the middle of it. Derrick tapped the cape twice with his wand, then opened the piece that he had cut, stuck his head in and looked around. "It's all clear. We can go through Sam; the distraction."

Sam made his pet ferrets collapse to the ground and turn to shades of blue. "Somebody help my ferrets Rocco and Sandy had collapsed. I think they're chocking on something."

All eyes gazed upon Sam as Reign and Derrick bolted into the men's bathroom through the portal they created with the cape landing in the men's restroom.

Once in the bathroom, Derrick hurried over to the door and peered out looking for patrol members in the area. "We can go in a few seconds."

"This is so exciting to be involved in this."

"It's dangerous. You don't have to do this."

"I know, but I m already involved."

"Good point. Three, two, one, go!"

Reign and Derrick ran down one of the halls adjacent to the main one. Derrick cupped his hand behind his ear. "Here that? That's Mr. Bishop pushing his cart. Hide."

They quickly hid in the shadows as Mr. Bishop rushed past them jotting something down on a cloth.

Mr. Bishop handed the cloth and a map to a mysterious figure standing in the stairway. Derrick couldn't make out who stood there, but as soon as he or she showed up, the mystery figure took off up the stairs as he finished reading the note. The note turned to ashes as the figure hid in a nearby vent.

Several patrol members marched toward Mr. Bishop who jetted away toward the exit. Patrol Member Seventy pointed his wand at him and stopped him in his tracks. Another patrol member handcuffed his hands behind his back while one confiscated his flute. The others took his cart.

Mr. Bishop fought to get loose from their grip as they walked toward the containment cells.

Derrick drew in a deep breath as Reign sighed. His eyes met hers. "Are you still in?"

"Yeah"

Derrick and Reign waited for a few seconds, then bolted over to the stairwell looking for the mysterious figure. Derrick nodded and shrugged his shoulders. "We've got to be careful and quiet."

They decided to go up a few levels and see if they could locate any clues lying. When they reached the top floor, a pile of ashes lay on the ground.

Derrick's eyes widened. "Well, how are we going to fix this problem?"

"Let me show you what I got. This is easy-peasy." She slipped out her wand, waved it around in a circle, tapped three times in the air, and watched as the note restored itself.

The mystery figured observed Reign from the vent.

"Nice going Reign." He retrieved the note. "I don't understand this language, do you?" He handed her the cloth.

Reign lifted the cloth. "It's in the language of Mr. Bishop, but lucky for you, I can read it."

"What are you waiting on? Read it, please."

"I didn't get the book in time. It is on its way to King Damarco with two Royal Patrol members, maybe more. P.S. My cover has been blown."

Derrick's jaw dropped. "Mr. Bishop was a spy, but for whom and why?" He put the note in his back pocket. "Add this to the list, but I still don't know how all of this tied in together."

"We've got to look around for clues and then hurry back to Mrs. Cat's class."

The two left for class.

The mystery figure waited for a few minutes before he decided to leave when the patrol members patrolling the hall with dogs approached him looking everywhere for anybody connected to the attempt to steal the *Red Wizard Book*.

The mystery figure needed to escape; he moved backward not making a sound inside the vent. Using the map, he discovered an alternative way out of the vent bypassing the patrol members. He arrived at Mr. Smith's door, walked over to him. "I need to give Barrett a note from his mother."

"Fine, just make it quick."

He approached Barrett with the message. Barrett took it from him.

The mystery figure left the room and stood next to the door.

Barrett read the message. "*Mom caught your blackbird in her food and put it in a cage. She sends the new gift back. Should I send your pets after it and keep the blackbird from talking?"*

The mystery figure waited at the door for the signal from Barrett, then took off on his mission.

Derrick and Reign made their way back to the bathroom and back through the mirror into their classroom right when Mrs. Cat returned. Derrick signaled to Sam with a thumbs' up.

Sam rubbed his ferrets' fur; they shook then stood up. "They're fine folks thank you everyone."

Reign grabbed her cape off the wall and stood next to Derrick.

Mrs. Cat stood in front of the class. "The principal has lifted the lockdown. When the bell rings, proceed to your next class."

Derrick leaned over to Reign. "With all the excitement, Mrs. Cat forgot she was going to turn me in for what I did at the Honor Museum."

"You live to see another day."

When the bell rang, he quickly hurried out of the room dunking in the crowd not to be seen by Mrs. Cat and headed to gym class. *My favorite class and I get to play mud ball.*

Derrick entered the locker room and strolled over to a locker near Charles, who finished changing his clothes.

"Hey Charles, are you ready for some mud ball?"

"Why is that?"

"Because your shoes are all dirty. You've been out getting ready for our match against the rich kids."

"Hmm. Oh…yeah, getting ready to crush those rich snobs."

"That's what I like to hear."

As the rest of the students dressed, a few of his classmates clowned around snapping towels at each other.

Mr. Cash entered. "Stop roughhousing. Get dressed and make it quick. You have two minutes, or you'll get five hundred pushups."

"Remember there are only two rules you need to know. Don't kill anybody and the first group to capture the other team's flag wins. This type of game usually gets out of control in a hurry."

The students stopped their horseplay and headed out to the field waiting for the rich kids to show. The sky turned partly cloudy. Occasionally the sun poked out from the clouds. The field large oval shape green pasture with trees, bushes and boulders provided the perfect spot for any sport. A sizable wall surrounded it.

A few moments later, the door swung open and a bunch of lackeys sprinted out followed by the rich kids. The rich kids ruled the school with their parent's money and didn't care if they hurt anybody on the way.

Mr. Cash blew his whistle. "Get into your teams, and let's begin the game." A few gnomes served as refs.

Derrick observed the rich kids who lined their lackeys up in front of them.

Seconds later, Mr. Cash raised his wand to the sky and released an energy flame which exploded and signaled for the game to begin.

Everybody bolted looking for cover behind the trees, bushes, and boulders. Charles and Derrick headed to their favorite spot to hide in this game. They watched as a lot of the front line of the rich kids' lackeys went down as well as a few of his classmates. Derrick searched the area for the location of Barrett and his crew. He found Barrett attacking from the south side of the field, capturing more of his troops.

Charles and Derrick already got to the rest of the rich kids by using the magic tricks they brought along. They quickly planned to beat Barrett and his lackeys. They decided to split up and attack him on both sides, with mud balls flying all over the place. One almost hit Derrick in the face as he slipped behind a tree. He watched as Charles fell onto the ground. Mud splattered six-feet high.

It eventually came down to Barrett and Derrick who stood in the middle of the field using their magic to win the game.

Derrick stomped the ground like a bull ready to charge. "You know I'm going to win this game again for the fifth time."

“Not if I have anything to do with it.” Barrett clenched his fists.

“Derrick you need less talk and more action if you’re so bad.”

Derrick whisked his hands. “Leaves of Mother Nature protect me in your arms and share my face.” The leaves fell around him into clones of himself to hide his movement from Barrett. He slipped away from the clones as they attacked Barrett. Derrick was ten feet from reaching the flag when the ground quacked; mud rose up in front of him forming a giant mud hand that jetted toward him. Barrett’s giant mud hands eliminated all of Derrick’s clones. He did all he could to avoid Barrett, but Barrett just kept charging.

Eventually, Barrett cornered Derrick, and he couldn’t block his attack which gave Barrett the victory. Right at that moment, Barrett walked over and stepped onto Derrick’s wand snapping it into pieces while blocking the heinous site of what he had just done from the class. A ton of emotion ran through Derrick all at once.

With a sly grin, Barrett kneeled by Derrick. “That is what you get for playing with the big boys.”

Derrick observed the rich kid’s celebration.

Barrett walked off the field waving the victory flag in his hand.

Derrick pounded the ground. *I want to knock his block off.* He stood and swiped the mud off his face.

Mr. Cash blew the whistle. The game now officially over haunted Derrick as he gazed upon his broken wand. *I might not ever be able to use this again.* He sighed a deep-boned heave as he wrapped his wand inside a scarf and then placed it inside his pocket then left for lunch.

7. Protect the Message

Earlier that day after getting the signal from Barrett to attack the Royal Patrol members responsible for delivering the *Red Wizard Book* to Sand Brook Wizard Academy, the mystery figure escaped into the forest behind the school and located a secure spot from the patrol members who looked for him. He reached into his coat pocket for his whistle to call forth one of his master's dark werewolves.

The mystery figure lifted his whistle to his lips and blew a high-pitched D-minor ascending melody. Nothing happened at first, then suddenly the sky turned dark gray. The wind increased quickly spreading thousands of leaves as if in a wind tunnel. Within minutes, a giant dark werewolf, maybe six feet tall with dark gray fur, athletic build, sharp canines, scars on ten percent of his chest, and with a stubbed tail stood proudly before him. The beast sniffed him. "I am Howling Fang. What can I do for you, sir?"

"Master Bloodstone needs you to retrieve the *Red Wizard Book* from the Royal Patrol members. You must retrieve it before they reach Sand Brook Wizard Academy. Take more dark werewolves with you for back up. Do this without anybody left alive."

Howling Fang nodded and then disappeared toward his mission. At that moment, the sky cleared up, and the wind calmed. The mystery figure hurried back to the school avoiding detection.

Howling Fang scampered into the forest moving at an exceedingly high pace releasing a howl that echoed across the land which called for his pack of darker werewolves to appear one after another until there were six. They sniffed the air.

"I smell the Royal Patrol; follow me." Howling Fang leaped toward an opening headed for the road.

The other dark werewolves followed without hesitation as if searching for prey. The pack eventually caught up to the Royal Patrol carriage.

"See, there they are." Howling Fang narrowed his eyes and flashed his sharp teeth. "Pull back and follow at a safe distance. When the time is right, you three take the left side of the carriage and you three take the right. We'll surround it and attack it."

Each werewolf howled in unison to acknowledge the plan. It only took minutes for Howling Fang to issue the howl charge. One of the dark werewolves leaped onto the Royal Patrol members who rode behind the carriage ripping them from their saddles and spooking their horses.

Royal Patrol Member Ten stopped the carriage in the clearing. "Patrol Member Seventy, you stay in the carriage and watch the *Red Wizard Book* with your life. The rest prepare yourself for a fight."

At that moment, two Royal Guards retrieved their silver-coated crossbows, while the others made silver-coated shields emerge as their wands transformed into swords.

The sky turned morbid, dark gray as the dark werewolf's howls rang out. Suddenly, the battle started. Loud clangs from swords and claws rang out all over the place.

"Clang! Scrap! Clang! Boom......Boom!" The blows to one another in the fight knocked down trees and bushes which ripped from the ground. Startled by the battle sounds, the horses took off with Patrol Member Seventy inside the carriage struggling to reach the door to exit. The wagon jerked forward fast sending her flying backward. The carriage raced out of control past everyone as if on fire.

Patrol Member Seventy climbed from the carriage and wrangled her way to the top. She grabbed the reins, pulled hard and tugged hard. "Whoa, Nellie." Eventually, the carriage slowed as she regained control of it. She glanced over her shoulder hoping the Royal Patrol members maintained the advantage during this battle. The carriage came to a stop.

She clutched the *Red Wizard Book* as she released one of the carriage horses and rode toward Sand Brook Wizard Academy.

One of the dark werewolves witnessed her departure but couldn't chase after her; his blood boiled over at the sight of her escape. The battle lasted for forty-five minutes until the final Royal Patrol member collapsed to the ground. Two of the six darker werewolves and all Royal Patrol members bodies scattered the battlefield the area.

Howling Fang and another Dark Werewolf realized the carriage took off. They split in different directions to locate it. One of them picked up the carriage's scent, and Howling Fang followed.

Only a half a mile into the forest, they found the carriage with the door open and no signs of the patrol member in it. They sniffed and picked up the direction of her scent.

The dark werewolves discussed their next step since they weren't supposed to have anybody live and to retrieve the book. Howling Fang glared at the other dark werewolf. "We have no choice. We must use magic and transform into Royal Patrol members who lay dead from the battle. Then we can carry out our master's plan."

Howls filled the air.

***

Meanwhile, on the way to the cafeteria, a group of fairies heading to lunch almost knocked down Derrick, but he ducked right in time. When Derrick entered it, his mom's assigned chair and the assistant principal's chair remained vacant. *Where is everyone? Where is my dad too?* He felt a queasiness crawl inside his stomach. *"This must be a result of Mr. Bishop's little ordeal in the hall earlier."* He glanced around the cafeteria. *Why does everyone sit in social groups? Mingle people, mingle.*

Derrick strode to stand lunch line, picked his items, and then took a seat at his usual spot next to Reign. *So much for mingling.*

"Hey, Knuckle Head." She flashed a smile.

"Oh, what's up Reign? Where did you come from?"

"What do you mean? I've been sitting here for minutes! You've been daydreaming for minutes, Derrick! So, did you hear that Barrett was offered a chance to go to Sand Brook Wizard Academy but decided to head to Waldorf Wizard Academy instead?"

"No, I thought he was thinking about going to Sand Brook Wizard Academy instead of Waldorf Wizard Academy."

"No, guess it's just us and a few others who will be attending Sand Brook tomorrow. Isn't that great?"

"Yep, that…is."

"Oh yeah, I'm still looking for info on the clues that we found. My friend has a tough time finding anything."

"What? You weren't supposed to tell anybody about that stuff!" Derrick abruptly stood.

"Don't freak out about that. He is cool; I told him not to tell."

"Are you sure we can truth him to keep our secret?"

"Yes, I'm sure."

Derrick sat down, pondered not having Charles around anymore and having to find new friends.

Charles walked over with his tray of who knows what and dropped it in front of Reign.

She glanced up from her lunch. "Is that all of it or is there another tray behind your back?"

Reign smiled as she observed Charles giving her a heinous facial expression while shoveling that so-called food into his mouth never coming up for air. She noticed Derrick not eating much. "I'm surprised you're eating what is on the menu today instead of a packed lunch."

He picked through his lunch and only ate his bread, an apple and two bites of bat stew. "I want something else. This food tastes awful."

"Why don't you just use your wand to change it, Derrick?"

"Did something happen to your wand at gym?"

"I don't want to talk about that right now. Let's talk about the school being on lockdown."

Twenty minutes later, the assistant principal entered, but no Mrs. Blackwell. Everyone stopped in their tracks and waited for Mr. Lion to walk down the aisle. He turned and faced the students. "Your principal, Mrs. Blackwell, wants me to apologize for her tardiness today. Something important came up that needed her full attention. That is the reason she put the school on lockdown. I also wanted to say that I'm incredibly happy for those who were accepted into Sand Brook Wizard Academy, Waldorf Wizard Academy, and the other academies. So, let's give them a big round of applause and wish them luck."

The students clapped and whooped and hollered gleefully.

Mr. Lion left the cafeteria.

Derrick finished his lunch. "I think I should go find my dad and speak with him. Maybe he'll have some answers."

Reign stood as she nodded in agreement. "I'll go with you."

"Not this time, but thanks. I think this is something I need to do on my own."

Reign's smile vanished as she plopped onto her chair.

***

Meanwhile, Mr. Bishop sat helpless tied to a chair in a containment area covered with special magic to stop captives from escaping. Beads of sweat poured from his forehead.

Two Patrol Members maintained a tight guard on him. Patrol Member Six glowered toward his captive. "It won't be long until Mrs. Blackwell arrives to interrogate you."

"It's hot in here."

"Now you know why it's called a hot seat."

Patrol Member Nine searched Mr. Bishop's cart to see if they missed any stolen items.

"I'm innocent."

"That's what they all say."

***

Across campus, Jacob escorted by a patrol member entered his wife's office. "Hey Kayla, is everything okay? Did you find the spy?"

"Yes, honey, we think it was Mr. Bishop. The patrol members put him in a cell downstairs. We were going to leave to interrogate him right as you walked through the door."

"Oh, okay." Jacob turned to leave but stopped. "If you need help with the interrogation let me know."

"Thanks, honey, but I don't think I need additional help with this matter."

"Understood. Just be careful."

Her eyes darted toward him as if ready to throw a fire flame.

"Okay, I'm out of here." He left as the assistant principal entered in the office along with Patrol Member Twenty-one.

He cleared his throat to announce his arrival.

"Well, is he the spy who was in my office earlier today?"

Patrol Member Twenty-one stepped forward. "Yes, there were traces of him in your office and the secret passageway,"

"Did you find any clues in his cart that would tell us what he was doing in here?"

"No."

"Let's assume that he was sent here for the book. Interrogate him to see if he'll tell us anything."

***

Mr. Bishop sat helplessly profusely sweating in the containment area; his chin to his throat and his eyes fixated on the floor. Suddenly, the tapping of Kayla's heels clicked down the steps filled the containment area as Mr. Bishop lifted his head.

She stood in front of him. "So, Mr. Bishop, what were you looking for in my office?"

"I was nowhere near your office today. You caught me in the hall; I repeat, I was nowhere near your office."

"Do you expect me to believe you after you ran toward the side doors?"

Patrol Member Twenty-one inched closer to Mr. Bishop. "Why did you hide your tracks that were coming from Mrs. Blackwell's secret passageway?"

"I don't know what you're speaking about. I was working in the school and became scared when I saw a bunch of patrol members running toward me. And, that's the truth."

"Who are you working for?"

"I'm not sure whom you are referring to? I'm not working for anybody. Are we done with these questions?"

"The longer I keep you in here to sweat it out, sooner or later you'll talk. Save yourself some pain and suffering and cooperate with me. Who hired you?"

Mr. Bishop glowered toward her. "Nobody. I am innocent."

Kayla glanced toward Patrol Member Sixty-seven. "Go get me some truth slugs from Mr. Blackwell. He'll know why."

"Of course, Mrs. Blackwell." Patrol member Sixty-seven left to retrieve the truth slugs.

"Mr. Bishop, you are not in a position to hide anything from me. I will get to the truth."

"If you're trying to scare me, it's not working. I'm trained."

"Trained in cleaning floors and to scrub toilets?"

"That's not what I meant."

"Then explain it to me, Mr. Bishop. I trusted you. We all trusted you. How could you go against everything we teach here? You're disgusting as an individual."

***

Patrol member Sixty-seven made it to the second floor and then proceeded to run down the hall to enter Jacob's lab. Jacob prepared for his last classes of the day when Patrol member Sixty-seven barged through the door out of breath. "Sir, Mrs. Blackwell needs some of your truth slugs. Do you have any?"

"Let me see. I usually keep the truth slugs in a safe spot inside my closet." Jacob unlocked his closet and retrieved a jar filled with the slugs. He handed it over to the Patrol member who bolted for the door to deliver them to Mrs. Blackwell. He arrived five minutes later with the slugs and handed them to her.

She smiled as she studied the slugs in the jar. "See Mr. Bishop; the truth will surface. Chain him down."

Several patrol members held Mr. Bishop as others chained him. He fought for a brief period but soon relinquished his fight.

Kayla advanced toward him unscrewing the top of the jar. "Speak now or forever hold your scream." She lifted one slug and placed it into Mr. Bishop's ear while Patrol member One held his head from moving.

The slug weaved its way into his brain and proceeded to attack. Mr. Bishop fought the slug for a while before it overpowered him.

"Now, Mr. Bishop, will you give me the answer I'm looking for from you?"

"Yes, Mrs. Blackwell, what do you need from me?"

"What were you doing in my office today? How did you know about the secret passageway?"

"I was looking for the *Red Wizard Book*. I used a path seeker map to guide me to your office."

"What dangers may we expect in the future, and who is your puppet master?"

"My master will come and take back what is his and put you people into slavery. My master is... my master...is." The slug effect wore thin.

Kayla hurried to place another truth slug into his ear, but right when she did the candles flames blew out. "Light them at once."

Once the patrol members relit the candles, Kayla glanced at Mr. Bishop. He collapsed and remained motionless. She checked his pulse and for air coming from his nose. "He's dead. He's been murdered. Search the school again for whoever killed Mr. Bishop. There is a conspiracy happening around us, and this is just another piece of a much bigger puzzle. We must inform the Royal Council immediately." Kayla ran up the stairs to her office and then wrote down what she'd just learned. "Rose, come."

Rose, her pet owl flew to Kayla landing on her desk. Kayla tied the note to her leg and released her. "Take this to Sand Brook Wizard Academy."

***

Derrick headed up the steps toward his dad's school lab. When he entered, Jacob ignored him as he concentrated on one of his wild projects. Derrick waited to see if his dad would notice him. After a moment, Derrick tapped his dad on his shoulder which startled Jacob and sent paperwork flying.

"Sorry Dad, I didn't mean to startle you like that. Just want to talk to you if you have time."

"I'm kind of busy, but I can give you a few minutes of my time. What do you want to talk about?"

"I wanted to ask you about something that's been happening around me and get some answers."

Right as Derrick was about to explain himself to his dad, Patrol member Thirty appeared at his door. "Excuse me, Mr. Blackwell, the principal has required your presence at once. Please report to the office as soon as possible."

"Great. Something always gets in my way when I'm dealing with my parents."

"Sorry Son, maybe we can talk about this later." Jacob left right away for the office.

Derrick headed for his last class of the day. Frustration filled him as he walked out of the room. He felt as if he wanted to break something. As Derrick walked down the hall toward his next class, he noticed Harry, the captain of the chess club and the teacher's pet rifling through his locker for books. He pushed Harry into his locker while locking it behind him. *That didn't help me much. Maybe a little.* He kept moving toward his next class - "105 Showmanship." Once school finished for the day, he ran to his locker to grab his bag and hoverboard.

He placed his hoverboard down, stepped onto it, and then reached for his wand. *Oh yeah, it's broken. I have to wait for the carriage for a ride home.*

While Derrick waited for the carriage, Charles swooped down from the sky and morph back into himself.

"Hey, Derrick. Why are you walking instead of flying?"

"My wand got crushed during mud ball compliments of Mr. Bloodstone."

"Oh, I forgot I heard about that. You okay?"

"I'm okay, but Barrett broke my wand in gym, and I don't have a lot of money to fix it."

"I know how you can fix your wand if you're interested, but you have to do a few things to have it done."

"How?"

"An old man named Uriah; he lives in the forbidden forest. He can fix your wand and increase your power, but you have to join his group."

"I don't know about doing that."

"Well, think about it and let me know later."

"Okay, well I'm off."

Charles morph back into a hawk and flew off in the sky toward his home.

The carriage ride home gave Derrick time to reflect on Charles' suggestion. *I must admit I am a little curious*. He finally arrived home after an hour and twenty minutes later; his parents still at the school.

8. The First Mistake

The pitch-black cold house seemed lonely to Derrick. *I hate it when I'm alone in this house.* Derrick lit the fireplace and all the candles throughout the living room and kitchen. As he strolled into the kitchen, he discovered a note from his grandma. Atlas greeted Derrick in the kitchen.

"We will be back later. There is some dinner in the icebox. P.S. Congratulations about getting accepted to Sand Brook Wizard Academy!" He placed the note back onto the counter.

Derrick moved to the icebox and looked in searching for a snack. To his dismay, his grandma didn't prepare a meal. He huffed. *Now what? I don't cook, and my wand is broken, so I can't magically whip up dinner.* He gave Atlas some Herring then grabbed slice bread with butter and went to his room.

While in his room, Derrick wrote the events that happened that day and the amount of money he would need to get his wand fixed. After that, he packed his clothes for Sand Brook Wizard Academy. When he finished, he lay in his bed and drew in his notepad designing new magic tricks and machines while petting Atlas until he dozed off to sleep.

Several pebbles knocked up against his window.

Derrick rubbed the sleep out of his eyes and walked over to the window. "Hey, Charles. What are you doing here?"

"Did you think about the conversation we had earlier? Do you want to get your wand fixed or not?"

"Yeah, maybe we can talk to Uriah about that."

"Well, can you sneak out tonight?"

"Hmm, let me see if my family is asleep."

Derrick strolled around the house peeking in everybody's room. His mom and dad slept, but his grandma in the front yard engaged in cauldron chanting spells with several other witches.

Derrick had to make it look like he was still in bed, so he grabbed a bunch of his dirty clothes and tucked them under his sheets to form an outline of his body.

Atlas woke up from his wild dream, right when Derrick reached the window. His ears lifted. "Where are you going?"

Derrick stopped in his tracks.

"I'm just going out with Charles tonight. Can you impersonate me if my mom or grandma shows up?"

Atlas thought for a minute and then agreed to do it for a favor. "Whatever it is, just name it. I'll owe you one."

"I will get back to you on the favor later."

Derrick used the vines next to his window to climb down from his room. As Derrick landed, he and Charles crept from the area until they reached a safe spot and then ran toward their destination.

As Sabrina chanted over the cauldron with her witch friends, she noticed two figures leaving from the side of the house. She left the group to check on Derrick.

Once up the steps, Sabrina knocked on Derrick's door and waited for an answer, but it never came; so, she opened the door. At that moment Atlas who hid under a pile of Derrick's clothes impersonated Derrick's voice.

"Mmmm, Grandma is that you in my room?"

"Yes, baby, I was making sure you were okay. Now go back to sleep."

As Sabrina left Derrick's room, Atlas turned, accidentally uncovering his tails. She yanked the sheet off the bed exposing Atlas. He sat there in shock and panic.

"I will deal with you later, but for now tell me where Derrick went."

"I don't know; he left with Charles five minutes ago."

Sabrina immediately left to find Derrick.

***

While running through the forest following Charles, Derrick wished he had his hoverboard along with him. His legs started to feel heavy, and Derrick wanted to stop, but he eventually spotted a carriage. "Wait! What's that doing out here in the middle of nowhere?"

"Uriah sends this carriage for you if you want it."

The mahogany brown carriage with steel handles, railing and steps seemed out of place.

Derrick's eyes narrowed. "Who are those two figures in monk's robes are nearby it."

"They're a few of Uriah's men don't worry about them."

"Are you sure." "Yeah, I'm sure."

Why am I looking around and contemplating if he should even get in this carriage.

Charles looked at Derrick. "If you want to open that well of power that you have plus fix your wand, this carriage can take you to Uriah who can help you. So, do you want to go or what?"

"Hmm…okay, let's go before I change my mind."

They made their way to the carriage. The driver nodded. "Get in, Uriah is waiting for the both of you."

They stepped into the carriage followed by the hooded man. The other robed men rode on the top of the carriage. As they rode off, Derrick noticed that the window's coverings made it hard for him to see out. Nerves pinched Derrick's throat.

Hot on the pursuit of Derrick, Sabrina kicked the side of her horse. "Silver, keep sniffing for the location of those two boys." Silver picked up their scent fast and tracked them to a dead end in the middle of the forest. She stopped, dismounted and examined the tracks that remained on the ground. Once Sabrina shifted the debris through her fingers, she held the debris for Silver to sniff. He sniffed twice in the air and then locked onto the scent of the carriage. Silver took off in its direction.

9. Born of an Enemy

As Derrick, Charles and the hooded man sat in the carriage, Derrick's mind filled with worry. *Am I doing the right thing?*

The Hooded man remained motionless guarding the exit.

Then, he smirked toward Charles, who sat calm and quiet, next to him. He gathered his nerves and slowed down his pulse.

The sounds of hoofs hitting the ground echoed throughout the air. The ride was unpleasant with all the bumps, rocks, bridges and streams they passed along the way. After two hours into their journey, they managed to get to their destination. The carriage door swung open.

The hooded man exited first then Derrick and Charles.

About fifty robed and hooded figures stood chanting by a big bonfire in a clearing. As Derrick and Charles approached the fire, the hooded figures stopped chanting and gazed upon them.

Derrick puckered his lips. *All I can see are eyes staring at me. I don't trust this.*

The hooded man led Derrick and Charles into a nearby cave. Two torches burned by the entrance. The hooded man grabbed a torch, and then led the boys down a few chambers which led to a dead end.

Inside the hidden chamber, Barrett sensed Derrick's approach, so he placed on his magical mask which changed his appearance and voice to his personification as Uriah.

The wall slid open and allowed Derrick and Charles to enter. As Derrick walked in, lots of candles of all shapes and sizes lit the area as well as Uriah's odd mix of wood and gold jagged mystical creature mask. Uriah sat in a huge Nordic chair at the end wearing a long burgundy coat with straps, brown pants and a glove on his left hand.

Uriah motioned for Derrick to come closer to him. When Derrick reached about four feet in front of him, Uriah raised his hand for him to stop. "That's far enough. What do you want from me?"

"I was hoping you could fix my wand as well as make me stronger."

"Are you willing to join our group and become a part of our family?"

Derrick swallowed. *This is what I've been looking for a long time from my parents, and now, someone is offering it to me on a silver platter. Should I trust him or not?*

"Let me give you a taste of what I can do. Place your wand on that stand."

Derrick placed his wand onto the stand and then stepped back two steps. He stood and observed as he enchanted the wand. "Wand before me, make yourself a new, and stronger than before."

Uriah's staff gradient glowed light blue as he tapped sections of Derrick's wand; the pieces reconnected on the stand.

"Now try out your wand."

Derrick lifted his wand. All at once a powerful surge of energy shimmered throughout his body. "Amazing. I feel like he could do anything."

"Choose a trick or spell you haven't mastered in school and perform it now with pride and glory."

Derrick traced an outline of a large hole in the middle of the room while shouting a spell from the *Red Wizard Book* he remembered from the first two pages of the book. "As I point thy wand make a transport to guide me to the secrets of the unknown. With the strength of a lion, the cunningness of a fox, the fierceness of the werewolf, and the power of a locomotive I command thee." Derrick's wand lit up as he aimed it toward the large tunnel.

"Interesting choice my young wizard."

Then the bright light of a massive steam locomotive came barreling down in the tunnel. "I did it?"

"Derrick shut that down before it barrels through us."

"I don't know how."

Uriah stepped in and used his staff to close the large tunnel.

Then suddenly, the power Derrick felt emptied; he felt weak. A confused look came over his face as he turned back toward Uriah.

"Okay, that is enough of a taste. What do you think about the power you just used?"

"That was amazing! How can I get more of that power?"

"You must join the Dark Society."

"Yes, I want to join you. I want more."

"We are pleased to hear that."

"What's next?"

"You must be initiated to prove your loyalty to the Dark Society."

"I'll do anything?"

"We want you to retrieve two items for us before the next full moon."

"Okay, what items and from whom?"

"The Royal Council."

"What? No way, man! I will get into so much trouble for that from my mom and dad. And, it could get me locked into jail or worse, banished to Avalon Island."

"Well, do you want this power or not?"

"Yes, I do, but not going against my parents or the Royal Council."

"Consider your decision wisely. Not everyone who enters my chambers is asked to join. There are many advantages to our Dark Society.

If I just retrieve these items without being seen maybe I won't get in trouble. "Yeah, I will get those items."

"That's great to hear my future brother." You will be visited by a person who will hand you a compass that will show you the location of the items. Here, use that energy I unlocked and bring me those items." He lifted his hand. "Derrick and

Charles, depart from these chambers and do not ever return unless you bring me the items I requested."

On the way out of Uriah's secret chamber, Charles reached in his pouch for sleep dust and tossed it on Derrick.

***

Earlier that night, after an hour or more riding through the forest, Sabrina arrived at the location of the carriage and dismounted from her horse. On the way to the camp, Sabrina spotted a group of dark werewolves patrolling the area. "Silver!" They hid in the bushes downwind so that they couldn't smell them. "Silver, I need you to distract the dark werewolves so I can get closer to the bonfire.

Silver bolted like a bullet firing from a gun.

After waiting for the four dark werewolves to chase after Silver, Sabrina stealthy moved closer to the camp but walked into a hooded, robed figure. She quickly disposed of him with hand-to-hand techniques, and then slid his body behind the bushes, slipped into his hooded robe as a disguise, and then proceeded to search for Derrick. Her heart races when she observed there was no sign of him in the area. *Something is wrong, and I was supposed to keep him safe.*

Silver ran and ran passed trees, shrubs, fallen trees and leaped over creeks and large boulders. Once he got far enough to allow Sabrina to get pass the dark werewolves, he when on the attack. Silver shook his fur at a high rate to charge it creating sparks from his fur. His speed increased as he ran toward a pack of werewolves leaping into the air while swiping with lightning claw down on two of them sending the two dark werewolves crashing back at the other werewolves.

Suddenly, the large bonfire turned to embers, and hooded figures surrounded Sabrina. She transformed her wand into a sword, pulled her hooded robe off, and prepared for battle. The hooded figures pulled off their robes and then transformed into dark werewolves.

The dark werewolves grew bigger, and their skin turned gray. Their ears, teeth, feet, and hands became enormous with sharp like razors for claws. As the dark werewolves circled Sabrina, she tried to back out of the area; more dark werewolves encircled her. "Silver! Silver come!" Silver came in a hurry and stood by her side. His hair stood on the back of his neck; fur still charged while his eyes locked on the dark werewolves. Silver waited for Sabrina's word to attack.

"Silver, kill!"

Silver attacked two of the dark werewolves with fangs and lightning claws killing both. Sabrina used her magic to chain two dark werewolves to a tree, then sliced off the head of one and stabbed the other in the chest. She transformed her sword into a long silver rope with a blade on its end. She spun it over her head then launched it at the seven other werewolves managing to kill four.

As dark werewolves started to fall, the remaining ones howled for backup. The werewolves funneled out of the cave like a disturbed beehive. They surrounded Sabrina and Silver, still in the mood to fight. Uriah walked out from the cave through the werewolves and stood in front of her.

"You need to place your weapons down now! Or, your grandson will die."

"Who are you?"

"I'm Uriah the Destroyer."

"What a clever little name."

"Why don't you place your wand on the ground."

"Uriah! Where's Derrick? If you hurt him, I will kill you."

"Ha ha ha! You're not in the position to make threats or demands, Sabrina."

"How do you know my name?" "I have my ways."

"Why not, Uriah? As I see it, I could reach you before your dark werewolves can attack me."

Charles appeared from behind Uriah holding Derrick's lifeless body and with a knife to Derrick's throat.

Sabrina's eyes widened as she lowered her sword. "Silver halt!" Silver backed down.

"How could you, Charles betray my Grandson like this, I gave you the benefit of the doubt and now look at you, you revolting little Crescent Elf."

"Get her out of here. I don't have to answer you."

Two hooded, robed figures placed handcuffs on her wrists and escorted her and Silver away.

10. The Message Arrives

Hours ago, Patrol member Seventy arrived at Sand Brook Wizard Academy; her horse out of breath on the verge of collapsing. They approached the front gate. "I'm Patrol Member Seventy with a special delivery."

"Where do you come from and what is the reason you're here?"

"I come from Seven Moon village." She showed her glowing crested palms to the gatekeeper. "Here is my proof of who I am. Agent Eight sent me here to bring the *Red Wizard Book* to the Royal Council. My patrol group was broadsided on the way here by dark werewolves. I need to talk to King Damarco now."

The gates swung open, and they ushered her to King Damarco's study. Royal Patrol Member Three greeted her. "Wait here. I'll retrieve the King."

Her eyes lit in awe of the King's study as she gazed upon the bronze fireplace, the oak mahogany furniture, books that ran along the wall and the family's portrait.

The bookshelf slipped open, and King Damarco entered as she bowed before him

"I hear that you and my Royal Patrol members got broadsided on the way here. Did any of them survive the attack?"

"I am not sure. I left after my horse was spooked and raced off toward the trees. They were still fighting when I left."

"We need to find out what happened to them." King Damarco called forward his top man, Royal Patrol member one and asked him to send out a group of Royal Patrol members to see if any men survived the ordeal.

Patrol Member Seventy reached into her leather satchel and pulled out the *Red Wizard Book* which wrapped in cloth and handed it to King Damarco

"Thank you for keeping the book safe. Please be my guest in the castle before you head back in the morning."

"That is exceedingly kind of you, my King. It has been a rather long journey." She bowed.

"Guards, escort our guest to one of our bests quarters and make sure she has plenty to eat."

Several Royal Guards escorted her from the study as King Damarco opened the pack. He flipped through the pages, then placed the book in a secret spot.

Right at that moment, Mrs. Blackwell's pet owl, Rose, flew into the castle and one of the Royal Guards rushed the message to King Damarco, which he, in turn, relayed to the Royal Council.

***

Meanwhile, as the group of Royal Patrol members rode, they approached the carriage driven by the dark werewolves disguised as members of the Royal Guard. To aid their masterplan, they rode on the top of the carriage after placing the dead patrol members inside the carriage.

"Hey there, are you two okay?" Royal Patrol Member Five stepped forward and sniffed them.

"Yeah, we barely made it out of there alive. The rest of us are dead."

Royal Patrol Member Five sensed something unusual and the odor coming from the Royal Patrol members seemed strange.

"Well, let's get you home so we can patch you guys up." The two disguised dark werewolves followed Royal Patrol Member Five back to the academy.

***

The next morning, Derrick confused rose from his bed and looked around the room. *That's strange. I don't remember coming home. How did I wind up here?* He shook his head and then rubbed his temples. *Wait!* The last thing I remember is blacking out while leaving Uriah's.

He sat up in his bed and looked glanced at his clock. Atlas slept at the foot of his bed. As Derrick removed the covers, he used magic to dress in fresh clothes. He briefly patted Atlas as he slept and proceeded to leave his room. “Feels like a brand-new day. I feel great!”

At the bottom of the steps, his smile turned to a frown as he realized no one was there to wish him well on his journey to Sand Brook Wizard Academy.

His dad left him a note attached to a new book bag. He stood as he read it. “Sorry son, for not being around for your big day and in general. We are both proud of you and hope you do well at Sand Brook Wizard Academy. Here is a new bag from mom and potion from my lab that might come in handy. The new hoverboard is from your grandma.”

Derrick’s emotions bounced all over the place from anger to sadness as he stood to wait for his ride to Sand Brook Wizard Academy. Soon, a Royal cherry wood carriage with brown accents throughout and the Royal Crest appeared from the forest with two steeds pulling it and stopped in front of his home.

An older brown man climbed down from the carriage, placed Derrick’s things in the back and assisted him in entering. Reign lifted a sweet smile toward Derrick. “Glad you’re coming with me.”

“I couldn’t have said that any better if I tried.”

The carriage stopped at six more homes before they headed toward the academy. When it arrived, they all took in a deep breath.

Derrick tapped Reign. “I hate early mornings. Why does school have to start at six-thirty?”

“I guess because it has always been that way.”

“The building and grounds are beautifully nestled in the hills. I’m looking forward to orientation.”

“Let’s do this?”

Everyone exited the carriage and admired the massive building. The campus buzzed about the new students who arrived. Head Mistress Rubski faced the assembly. “Everyone proceed to the cafeteria for a briefing.”

The faculty advisor assigned Derrick to share a room. One of his roommates introduced himself, followed by another. The faculty gave new jackets to the new students and then, instructed them to place their green moon pendants onto them.

Head Mistress Rubski stood at the podium to make an announcement. “New first Semester Hawk and Semester Owls students, if you perform with greatness during their first-year semester, will receive an owl or a hawk as a reward. To heighten your goals, the top students will receive a guardian animal. Do your best work and put everything you learned into it. We do not allow those you do not perform or those who slack off to remain as a member of this academy. Do not disappoint me. Each new student has been assigned another student to show you to your dorm rooms. Dismissed.”

A senior student showed Derrick and Reign to their dorm rooms. When Derrick stepped in, he found an empty bed and placed his bags down and his hoverboard next to it. Just as he sat down, a knock at the door sent him bolting for it. A massive smile crossed his face when he saw a female student, five feet five, with light skinned and very pretty.

“I'm Robin. Welcome to the academy. I'm going to give a tour of the school; do you want to tag alone and scope it out?”

“I'd love to join you. Thanks for the invite.”

***

As the two disguised dark werewolves patrolled the academy, they found it exceedingly difficult to keep from attacking the other Royal Patrol members. The thirst for blood grasped the tips of each of their taste-buds. They smelled the book in the area but couldn't locate it. “I can sniff it.”

“Me too. It's hidden extremely well.”

While walking down a hall, Royal Patrol Member Nine approached them. “Report to the Royal Council immediately.”

They looked at each other puzzled. “Where?”

“In Wisdom Hall.”

“Oh, yeah; which way to Wisdom Hall?”

"That way. Come on; I will take you there. You guys must have really gotten hurt out there. You act like you've never been here before."

They arrived in front of the Royal Council as King Damarco's eyes fixated on them. "Tell me what happened in the forest."

"We were ambushed. We're lucky to be alive."

"Thank you for your actions. You two were a tremendous help in keeping the *Red Wizard Book* safe. Dismissed."

On the way out, they sensed the *Red Wizard Book* in the area.

King Damarco narrowed his eyes as he sensed something fishy about the two Royal Patrol members. "Royal Patrol Member Fifty-four, tail those two who I just dismissed. I'm concerned about the future of our people."

"With my lives, my King."

"I just received a message from Royal Patrol Member Eight. She informed me that Mr. Bishop was the spy, but she didn't find who was pulling his strings before he died. Plus, having Royal Patrol members attacked in the forest by dark werewolves makes me feel uneasy. Let's take this message seriously and start training more patrol members and heightening guards."

King Canon rose. "King Damarco, I advised about this extreme action and asked for more evidence before proceeding."

"We don't have time. We must protect the Kingdom and our villages."

"I believe the Royal Council needs to know for sure who is behind this before we take a serious mistake, we cannot take back.

King Damarco stood with authority. "You have heard my decree. Your comments are noted, King Canon."

11. The Wrong Move

Meanwhile, for the last month and a half at Sand Brook Wizard Academy, Derrick learned many new magic tricks and enjoyed most of the teachers, but in the back of his brain, he knew that the new energy that Uriah gifted him kept him on the mission at hand.

As Derrick sat on his dorm bed to study, he heard a double-tap on his door. A note slipped beneath it, he walked over to it then looked around to see if his roommates had woken. A hand-written message across the note caught his attention. *Read over a candle, then destroy note.* Once he held it over the candle, the hidden message appeared. *Meet me in the bathroom in five minutes and come alone.*

Derrick adjusted his pillows and blankets on his bed to establish the appearance that he was sleeping in it. He grabbed his bag before leaving. With his wand to guide him through the unfamiliar and dark halls of the Academy, he stealthy made his way past the pictures on the wall whose eyes seem as if they watched him as he passed.

Suddenly, lights drifted from afar, so he quickly hid in the shadows rapidly powering down his wand. He held his breath as two Royal Patrol members patrolled the area. Once the two Royal Patrol members turned the corner, Derrick hustled toward the bathroom dodging more Royal Patrol members lurking in the hall. When Derrick entered the bathroom, a voice came from somewhere in the bathroom, and then a shadowy figure appeared.

"Are you Derrick?"

"Yes, I am. Why don't you come close and stop hiding in the shadows?"

"I don't take orders from you! Let me see your arm, Derrick." The figure inched his way from the shadows, but not entirely.

Derrick pulled back his sleeves one at a time until he revealed his birthmark on his arm. A small package appeared on the sink in front of him.

"Uriah sent me to give you this package. It is supposed to help you with your mission. I hope you know what you're getting yourself into."

"What does that mean?" Derrick opened the package which revealed a chain with a compass attached to it. "I've seen this once before in the *Book of Honors*. This was King Damarco's compass that he wears around his neck, but how did you get a hold of it?"

"Read the inscription, Derrick." The shadowy figure vanished.

He lifted the compass to the light and read out loud. "If you are royalty or worthy of this compass, drop some of your blood upon it to unlock the power." He looked around first, then bit his thumb to retrieve some blood - one drop, then two drops of his blood splat on the top of the compass which opened it up before him.

Derrick's jaw dropped in shock. "Now we're talking magic. Compass, point me in the direction to the location of the crystal keys." He reached into his bag for a map to see what was in that direction. "Oh man, it's in the direction of the Forest of No Return. I don't like the way that sounds." He grabbed his bag and hoverboard and took off toward the Forest of No Return. *I've heard stories of people never returning from there.*

After weeks of surveying Sand Brook Wizard Academy, Derrick discovered a route to leave the Academy unseen. He picked a wall on the east side of the castle with a big enough window to avoid detection by any Royal Patrol members. At midnight, Royal Guard Twenty usually left his post for at least ten minutes. Derrick maneuvered passed the Royal Guards on the way to the east side of the castle. He waited in the shadows until Royal Guard Twenty took his short break. Once he left, Derrick bolted to the ledge and looked over. "Yikes, those stone spikes on the bottom could hurt somebody. Somebody like me."

The wind howled and as it whipped Derrick's hair. Derrick felt nauseous as he stepped out onto the ledge, but he descended the side of the castle, anyway. "Now this takes guts!"

As Derrick scaled the side, he lost his grip fell. "I'm too young to die." He managed to regain his hold and eventually landed safely onto solid ground. With his trusty hoverboard, he flew low until he felt safe enough to fly higher.

He landed in the Forest of No Return two-and-a-half hours later into the overgrown and thick greenery. "I've got this." Derrick transformed his wand into a sword. While slicing his way through the greenery, he sensed something or someone following, so he increased his speed through the forest toward one of the Crystal Keys. He arrived at an opening in the greenery, and his compass pointed to an old temple covered by big spiky skunk vines. With his compass in his hand, he used it to guide. The path proved more difficult than he expected.

As he walked around the temple using the compass to guide him, Derrick stepped onto a section of the floor which set off a trap of arrows. He darted one way and then to another flipping each time to avoid the onslaught of arrows. From then on, showed more awareness for his surroundings on guard for more deadly traps.

The compass guided him to a massive room with a hill filled with greenery; and sitting right in the middle on the top the crystal key stood proud and tall. As Derrick stepped toward the greenery, it shifted and, then transformed into a huge Shambling Mound beast heading straight toward him in a hurry. He couldn't get of the way quick enough as the mound pressed Derrick against the wall knocking his sword to the floor. "Sword, come!" His words short because Derrick could hardly breathe.

His sword immediately flew to him. Derrick sliced off the Shambling Mound's right arm that pinned him to the wall. The beast released his grip and backed away from Derrick.

The beast's arm grew back to Derrick's dismay.

Derrick caught his breath. He needed a distraction to reach the crystal key. He summoned his magic to launch a giant cobra made of fire to surround the Shambling Mound sending the beast into a panic mode.

Derrick quickly bolted around the beast, climbed a vine up the wall, and leaped onto him while grabbing the crystal key on the way down. As he hit the ground, he sprinted toward the exit.

The beast shot a jet of water out of his mouth at the cobra which extinguished it within seconds. The animal galloped after Derrick, shooting deadly needles.

Derrick dodged the onslaught and then collapsed at the entrance of the temple. His heart pounded hard as he stared at the disaster and stuffed the crystal key into his pack back. He hopped on his hoverboard and used the compass to guide him to the next crystal key. It pointed southeast as he flew, so Derrick steered his board in the direction of the compass indicated.

***

Barrett impatiently waited for his spy to return with news of Derrick's progression.

Charles entered the area. "Sir, Derrick has retrieved the first crystal key. He is on his way to the next one."

"Good, haha."

"What should we do, my Master?"

"Round up a group of dark werewolves and bring me those items. After you have them in your possession, thank Derrick in our unique way."

"Consider it done, my Master."

***

When Derrick got close to his destination, his stomach growled. "It's got to be past seven. It's been hours since I last ate." He decided to land a mile and a half away and hoof it to avoid Royal Patrol members.

"Sweet and juicy, red or green make a red juicy apple come to thy." His eye widened as the apple appeared in his hand. He took a bite of the succulent red apple and a swig of his jug of water. He pulled out his map to study the area and to determine what else was around him. *Wow, the only thing in this is the Honor Museum.* He placed the map back into his bag and attached his hoverboard to the back continuing with his mission.

Derrick ran through the forest, jumped over fallen logs, ran through a stream, and slid into a small valley. On the way toward the Honor Museum, he covered his face with a mask. It took him twenty minutes to approach the borders. He hid behind the bushes and observed the Royal Patrol members inspecting the area. *Getting that second crystal key isn't going to be easy.*

He reached into his bag and retrieved a potion labeled – "Invisible Potion." *Thank you, Dad, for this gift.* He poured half of the tube onto himself. He waited several minutes for the potion to take effect knowing that in thirty minutes it would wear off. After double checking the map, he proceeded to use the compass to guide him past the Royal Patrol members.

Derrick finally made it to the building after twenty-five minutes getting around booby traps, dogs and Royal Patrol members. The large wooden door at the Honor Museum had a round hole in it. It looked big enough to fit his compass, so he placed it into the hole. Suddenly, the compass lit up, and the door slid open. He quickly ran inside and grabbed the compass closing the door before the Royal Patrol members headed back that way.

On the way down the stairs, Derrick avoided the picture of cats on the wall and noticed that the invisible potion had started to wear off. First, his bag appeared. He quickly headed behind a big vase to the left of him. His compass pointed toward the guarded hall in the room at the end of the hallway. He waved his wand. "Oh, great door which holds such secrets, when I approach unlock for me."

Derrick ran forward and slid his bag between the two Royal Patrol members, which distracted them for a moment. Two ropes popped out of his bag and wrapped around both Royal Patrol members. Derrick waved his wand. "I say vanish and begone, you rats!" The guards transformed into rats and scurried off.

He bolted down the hall to the room as the potion wore thin. Derrick came to an abrupt halt. Just in front of him, the walkway ended at a dark deep pit full of spikes. *That was a close call! I almost fell into a pit of spikes. Now, where is that item*?

He used his hoverboard to fly to the second crystal key, which sat on a big spider web in the center of the pit. While flying, he looked around for the spider but didn't see it at first. When he reached for the crystal key, a giant black widow appeared and attacked him with intent to kill. He found it hard to avoid the jaws of the giant black widow, which stabbed him twice in the arm and sliced up his clothes. With all this happening, he managed to get stuck in the black widow's web. Before she could finish wrapping him, Derrick used his wand to glow brightly as the sun to blind the black widow, and then cut himself free from the web. With the black widow distracted, he used his magic to cut the webs beneath her which sent her crashing down to the spikes.

As he lifted the crystal key, an alert went off. Derrick quickly landed his hoverboard, threw the last crystal key into his bag, and took off toward the exit. Once Derrick was out in the hall, a vast group of Royal Patrol members stood in front of him with their wands drawn. He raised his arms in the air while handcuffs appeared around his wrists.

Royal Patrol member Ten walked over, and pulled off the mask from his face, and then stood in shock. "I thought you were smarter than this Derrick and would not head down this road. Your family will be extremely disappointed in you."

A few Royal Patrol members walked Derrick to a carriage for his transportation back to Sand Brook Wizard Academy to stand in front of the Royal Council in the morning. The path seemed long as Derrick walked toward the carriage from the Honor Museum. His grandma's disappointed voice echoed in his head, and Derrick lowered his head in shame. Right at that moment, a howl rang out, then several more. They stood ten feet away from the carriage when the first set of dark werewolves appeared from the trees and bushes and attacked.

Sirens rang out all around him; all Derrick wanted was to look for cover, but Royal Patrol member Ten still controlled him.

Mayhem erupted as a black crow flew down from the carriage and morph into Charles. He stabbed Royal Patrol member Ten in the back with a blade.

"Well…w…. ell, Uriah thanks you for retrieving these items. Uriah wanted me to tell you we no longer need your service. Oh yeah, and he wants back the power that he gave you."

"Wait, you're just going to step on our friendship like this and double cross me you jerk! I'm the one that made you relevant at Seven Moon High School. Without me, nobody would give you the time of day!"

"Well, let me start by saying thank you, but I've always been tired of being in your shadow. Now that I'm not, I just wanted to say good riddance to our friendship." Charles raised his arm and revealed an unfamiliar staff.

Derrick's body felt weak as Charles took back the power and then took some of Derrick's blood. After twenty seconds, Derrick collapsed onto the ground, and he passed out.

12. The Ugly Truth

Back at Sand Brook Wizard Academy, after two weeks of learning King Damarco's routine, the two disguised Royal Patrol members put their plan into action. While King Damarco and his wife Queen Gabriella took their nightly stroll around the Academy, the two disguised Royal Patrol members rummaged through the Royal suite until they found their secret room. They snatched the *Red Wizard Book*, but King Damarco and a few Royal Patrol members burst through the door before the disguised thieves could shimmy through the window.

"I command you to stop. Put down the book. Who are you, and what do you want with it?" King Damarco's face turned furious.

The thieves stopped in their tracks. "It's none of your business."

"I know for sure you're not leaving here with that book. If you try, you will meet the fate of death."

The two disguised Royal Patrol members grew larger as their clothes ripped from their bodies revealing their hairy dark wolf body. Their facial features broadened and transformed into the wolves as their sharp claws like metal and tails sprouted. The small werewolf flicked his tail. "You know I was getting tired of disguising myself as a revolting Royal Patrol Member?" He launched toward the King and his Royal Patrol members.

Royal Patrol Member Seven stepped in front of his King blocking the dark werewolf's claw with his blades while Royal Patrol Member five used his ax and sliced off his head.

The Howling Fang escaped through the window landing on tree branches several stories below.

The King raised his hand toward the window. "Retrieve the *Red Wizard Book*.

***

Derrick awakened at nine in the morning inside a holding cell. He searched the area for his wand, jacket and book bag. *They're not here. They confiscated them.* Scared, mad, and ashamed of last night's behavior he cupped his head into his hands. *I trusted Charles, and he ended up stabbing me in the back. Why Charles? Why?*

After fifteen minutes, he paced in front of the thin stone bed. Footsteps echoed throughout the hall headed his way. Two Royal Patrol members soon glared at him. The leaner one twisted his lips. "The Royal Council will see you now."

The cell door opened as a lump pinched Derrick's throat.

***

After thirty minutes answering questions in front of the Royal Council, Derrick waited for his judgment and sentencing. Derrick's parents sat frantically. Jacob looked at Kayla. "Where did we go wrong?"

"This isn't on us; it's on him. It was his action that gave the Royal Council the ammunition they needed."

"I wish they would delay their decision until we have time to discuss what happened with him."

"That won't happen."

The presiding Royal Council member slammed his gavel. "Derrick Blackwell you are hereby banished as your punishment."

"To where?"

"Avalon Island."

Derrick fell to the ground, placed his head between his legs, and wrapped his arms around them as tears streamed down his cheeks. *Avalon Island! Folks say it's hard to return from that island. Most die from trying to escape the island or from being alone, or worse, eaten by a deadly animal. There was only one person who escaped from the Island, but he went insane.*

His mother sobbed as she hid her face into her husband's shoulder.

"Guards! Escort the guilty to Wisdom Hall and prepare him for banishment."

Two Royal Patrol members escorted him into the Wisdom Hall, the Royal Council surrounded him and collectively used their powers to send him away as a blue shimmer covered Derrick.

***

In the forbidden forest, Charles arrived into the cave with the two crystal keys proudly presenting them to Barrett. Not long after an enormous grin developed on Barrett's face as he gazed upon Howling Fang standing in the opening of the room. The beast stumbled forward as blood dripped from his arm. He grasped tightly to the *Red Wizard Book* in his other hand. "Master, here is the book you requested. I fulfilled the mission."

"What took you so long to retrieve this book?"

"We had a tough time getting a hold of the book; we had to infiltrate the academy to get it." The dark werewolf snarled.

"What? I told you not to show yourself to anyone. You fail me?"

Barrett held his palm toward Howling Fang and used his magic to force his pet to his knees.

"But Master, I did retrieve..." The beast gasped for breath. "I retrieved the book. I did not fail you!"

With a flick of his hand, the *Red Wizard Book* shot to Barrett. "Now we are ready to bring back Samuel. You're lucky I still have a use for you, or I would kill you for sure. Leave my sight. You disgust me."

13. The Wild Card is Shown

Over on Avalon Island, Derrick's body gradually shimmered onto the beach as his banishment from the Royal Council began. Confused he glanced at his surroundings. He took a deep sigh. *I'm in the middle of nowhere.* He looked around again. *I think I'm surrounded by Seven Moon; it kind of looks familiar.* His lips formed a slow pout. *My life spiraled out of control.*

First things first, he remembered a story his grandma told him about how his grandpa survived weeks on end in the wild. *I remember grandma. Find water, food, shelter and build a fire.*

He weaved a basket out of banana leaves and retrieved water from a cold stream. After he dug for insects, grub worms and collected mushrooms and berries to eat, he built a shelter out of twigs and large leaves. He dug a pit, loaded it with wood and straw. "Now the hard part; get the fire started." He surveyed the area and located to flint rocks. *Perfect.* After he banged the stones together, several sparks ignited the fire. Day after day he survived by finding his food although it proved tedious work. *I long for grandma's cooking, even her stew.*

His clothes quickly tore and became filthy. The strong stench he failed to notice because he grew to ignore it. He eventually had to face the facts. He could either stay in his current location or try to find better accommodations. Move on Derrick, he told himself.

As he walked miles through the thick brush, avoiding wild plants and wild animals, he stumbled onto a campsite. To his amazement, an old man sat by a fire carving wood. The old man had hazel eyes, muscular arms, and long black braid hair with a strap of white in the front continued carving as if he had no care in the world. He sported a goatee and wore animal pelt as clothes.

Derrick remained hidden for a few seconds taking in the sight of the tree hut. The smell of fish cooking on the fire drifted his way. His mouth watered as he stared at the fish anticipating the mouth-watering taste. He stepped forward trying to stay quiet but climbed onto a branch and cracked it. Snap!

The old man didn't budge. "Derrick, I have been waiting for you to arrive. It took you long enough."

How does he know my name? Derrick's brow furrowed.

"Because I felt your aura as you approached. I am your Grandpa, Jarvis Blackwell."

"Grandpa! I must be hallucinating from lack of proper food and water."

"I am as real as real can be. Don't be afraid."

"How can I believe you? You have been missing or dead for years."

"We have the same type of scar on our wrist." Grandpa pulled up his sleeve to show Derrick. "See? Plus, the wand you carry around, I made it for you and engraved it with the words 'Young Prince of Dragons.' Now, do you believe me?"

"It could be a magic trick or my mind playing tricks on me."

"Why don't you come over here and try some of this fish? I can hear your stomach. Please, join me."

Derrick hesitated. "What did he have to lose banished to this terrible place? Beats where I've been." He took a seat across from his grandfather.

"I'll begin by telling you about myself, grandson."

"Grandson, that has a nice ring to it."

They spent the next hours getting to know each other swapping stories.

14. Unleashing the Truth of a Villain

ELsewhere outside the caves of the Dark Society, Barrett placed the two crystal keys on the fabricated altar. He poured Derrick's blood onto the crystal keys, then chanted words from the *Red Wizard Book*. "With the blood of a Goldenash, shall the Dark Void open its floodgates here in this mystical land." The moon turned a pale pink as the ground beneath Barrett's feet rattled. "Make thy presence known from the Dark Void."

From the Dark Void, Samuel appeared wearing a trench coat with cut off sleeves onto the fabricated altar from the Dark Void. Samuel gazed up and down at his five-foot-nine-inch body and his light skin. He rubbed his fingers through his dark blonde hair as his crystal-blue eyes stared upon Barrett.

Barrett kneeled as did the rest of the Dark Society. "Grandfather, I grant you the treasure of the *Red Wizard Book*." He handed Samuel the book. "I'm glad to see you have arrived intact."

"You have pleased me and brought honor to the Dark Society."

"Then we shall celebrate your return. We have prepared a feast fit for a king in your distinguished honor."

"Make it so. Soon after we'll march on the surrounding village, Seven Moon and Sand Brook Wizard Academy. Where is your Grandmother?"

"She is head of Waldorf Wizard Academy now. We will see her in several weeks."

Samuel lowered his hand. "Kiss my crested ring to honor my return and shout my name throughout the land that I have returned."

Barrett obeyed kissing the crested ring. "Let's feast to celebrate!"

***

King Damarco sat at his desk table scribing a message to a neighboring village leader. "I bring to your village worrisome news regarding Samuel. He has been released through the Dark Void; and if our villages are to survive, we must join forces and ready for war. I will send you all of the Royal Patrol members I can spare to help protect your village.

He rolled the note and tied it to the leg of his faithful hawk Cham. "Now fly. Let all the village leaders under our protection be notified."

***

Back at the Blackwell home, Atlas lay on Derrick's bed napping as the sun pierced through the curtains and dispersed along one of his tails. As he moved his tails from the sunlight, a messenger sparrow landed on the window seal. It continued to chirp until Atlas rose and took the letter from his leg. The sparrow took flight.

Atlas morphed his paws into hands to read the note. *The King and Queen order you to immediately return home to Turqua Village.* He morphed his body until he reached four feet eight inches, his head increase, with his fangs and claws. He licked his fur down and straightened whiskers. Atlas reached under Derrick's bed for his belt, cape, and his magical bo staff. He bolted down the stairs and out the front door. Atlas stopped at the side-yard well, reached into his belt and retrieved a mystical traveling coin flipping it in the air. It slowly tumbled deep into the well. Once the coin splashed into the water, Turqua village's reflection appeared in the water. Atlas jumped up onto the well and jumped in transporting to the village as instructed.

***

Back on Avalon Island after hours of conversing with his grandson, Jarvis stood. "So, Derrick, are you ready to change your ways and step forth to protect Seven Moon and the world?"

"What do you mean by that, Grandpa?"

"You were meant to protect Seven Moon. It is your destiny to defeat Samuel and Uriah."

"Yes, I want to change Grandpa."

"If you want to defeat them, you'll have to work on elevating your power. We have a lot to accomplish. You're lucky because two weeks in here equals two months out there."

Over the next couple of months, Derrick trained harder than he had ever prepared in his life under his grandfather's supervision and mastery. Every muscle in Derrick's body hurt from the challenges and obstacles Jarvis placed in front of him to accomplish.

"Grandpa, I can't do this anymore."

"Derrick, you can, and you will succeed. Now get moving. You have a world to save."

"Grandpa."

"Remember you're doing this for your family in Seven Moon. You're the only one who can and will defeat Samuel and his Dark Society. Now do the challenge again and beat your own record."

Derrick took a deep breath and jumped onto a limb and ran the obstacle pendulum for the thirtieth time.

***

The wave of Samuel's dark werewolves overwhelmed Seven Moon that it seemed as if they blacked out the sky. Soon most villages fell as if a swarm of bees covered them. If something did give quickly, within weeks Samuel's dark wolves would control the villages.

As Kayla stood in front of Samuel, she fought to free herself from his hooded men's grip. Jacob suffered from the same fate at her side.

Samuel smirked as he narrowed his eyes. "Well, well, well, who do we have here? Is that young Kayla Blackwell? You're all grown up. Jacob, it's nice to see you too my old student."

Kayla recoiled at the sight of Samuel. He licked his finger and then wiped it across her face. "Now, now, now, Kayla, I know you have more manners than that to show to your elders. I just wanted to thank your son, Derrick, for helping me escape from the hell hole that you helped put me in like a common thief."

Kayla spat three times onto Samuel's face.

"Just ill manners." He turned away from Kayla as he wiped the spit from his face with his handkerchief. He looked at the rest of the villagers. "You folks only have two choices. You can join the Dark Society or die!"

Kayla spat again. "We'd rather die than live under the rule of you or the Dark Society."

***

The autumn November day in Turqua Village presented as a glorious change of colors compared to Seven Moon as Atlas arrived through a well on the outskirts of the village.

"I'm wet enough without it raining." Atlas shook his body to rid his fur of the excess wetness. He tilted his nose and sniffed the smell of the large lemongrass trees which drifted in the breeze.

A white cat with black spots meowed. "Welcome home my lord, the smell of lemongrass trees are very lovely around this time of year. Don't you think?"

Atlas glanced at the cat, which held the door open to a black cherry oak short carriage with a Shrub deer harnessed to it.

"Yeah, it is my humble servant."

"The King and Queen are waiting on you." "Okay, on we go then. We can't keep them waiting."

Atlas jumped into the carriage, and they proceeded to the Turqua Village which took ten minutes to reach the intended destination.

The Turqua felines pranced and hissed as the Warrior cats suited up for war. Commander Cole, an orange and black Warrior cat with part of his left ear missing, approached the carriage and waited for Atlas to exit.

"Atlas, it's good to have you home."

"I'm glad to be here, just not under these circumstances."

The cats embraced.

"This way my Prince. We must make our path to Warrior Summit for a meeting with King Nile and Queen Ebony."

"I'm right behind you."

When they arrived at Warrior Summit to see King Nile and Queen Ebony, stood at a granite table studying a map.

Atlas approached them and bowed. "My Lord, you summoned for me?"

The King glanced up from the maps and nodded. "Yes we did. It is nice to see you home son, your maturing well. I see the Blackwell family has been taking good care of you."

"They have, and I thank them for that, but I know you didn't call my home for that." "No, we are preparing for battle as you can see Atlas."

"A battle with whom my Lord?"

"You haven't heard?"

"No!"

"Samuel was released from the Dark Void weeks ago, and now he's marched through villages destroying them with the help of Uriah and the dark werewolves led by Howling Fang."

"How did Samuel get free from the Dark Void? I helped place him in there years ago."

"I heard Derrick Blackwell helped release him."

"I can't believe my ears, my Lord. Derrick wouldn't do such a thing as that."

"But he did, and he's now banished to Avalon Island."

"What? This cannot be real."

"I know you're close with him Atlas, but right now you have to focus on your Turqua Felines. I've got word that Uriah and Samuel are heading this way. I fear battle is near and we don't have much time to prepare the Warrior cats."

Atlas flicked his tails. "Then we shall prepare to defend our land? Guards protect the King and Queen with your life and place them in the secret room."

A Warrior cat entered the area. "I have a message Commander."

"Are the felines citizens safe?" Commander Cole furrowed his brow.

"Yes, my Lord."

Atlas followed Commander Cole out of Warrior Summit before the alarm bell went off. He took off his magical bo from his back, spun it, and then tipped it to the ground. The yellow willow flowers lit up and released spores into the air creating an invisibility shield around Turqua Village and felines in the area.

"Take the King and Queen to safety." Atlas bowed toward the King and Queen as several Warrior cats escorted them to safety. "Warrior Brigade Alpha, guard the right of the city. Brigade Beta to the left, Brigade Delta you're with me. No one makes a move without a direct order from me."

The warrior cats scattered.

Samuel, Uriah, Howling Fang and a group of Dark werewolves thundered toward Turqua Village like a herd of running buffalo. The shield around Turqua kept them at bay for a moment.

Samuel stood proud and ready for battle. "Come out, come out wherever you are warrior cats. I see you're hiding, is that the way of a warrior cats?"

The warrior cats lurked in their positions and waited for Atlas to signal for them to commence battle.

Uriah pursed his lips as he lifted his hands. "Dark werewolves find them and destroy."

The dark werewolves scattered as they sniffed as if on a hunt. Howling Fang howled to energize the others. "Samuel, we can't find them yet, but we won't stop until we do."

"Seek and destroy!"

Atlas released a sparrow, and the warrior cats attacked the dark werewolves as they pelted them to and fro. Smash! Hiss! Howl! Bang! Splat! Nothing but fur balls filled the area as they targeted and muddled Samuel's army.

Samuel lifted his wand. "Magic wand lift this spell; make the cloak disappear."

Atlas noticed the wind slowly increased gradually until the fierce wind blew the spores away from the village.

Although the warrior cats maintained control of the battle, they soon became outnumbered as the second wave of dark werewolves rampaged into the action. Smash! Hiss! Howl! Bang! Splat!

Atlas glared toward Samuel. "Warrior cats retreat. Live to see another day."

Howling screams from the felines erupted as they scampered from the decimated.

Atlas turned towards Turqua village. It almost seemed as if a tear fell and all appeared to be over with the warrior cats on the losing end of this battle. "We can't give up. There's always another way when magic is involved." He retrieved magic wild berries from one of his pockets and chewed it, then tossed one to the two warrior cats near them. Atlas' strength and speed increased as he and two warrior cats charged toward Samuel surrounding him while Atlas slammed his magical bo into Samuel's head knocking him to the ground and thirty feet into through trees. "Take that Samuel."

Samuel stood raising his staff and pointed it toward the wild vines. They whipped and wrapped around the legs of the two warrior cats. "Now cats turn to stone."

Gradually the two warrior cats became rock statues.

Atlas dodged the wild vines which caused Samuel to swirl his staff to make the wind slice into Atlas' fur sending him flying for miles before he crashed into a massive boulder knocking him unconscious.

15. The New Plan

The next day on Avalon Island, Jarvis woke his grandson from his sleep. "Derrick, Derrick, wake up, it's time to get back to training."

Derrick rolled over and rubbed the crusted sleep out of his eyes. "Not that I want too, but I know I gotta do it."

"That's right; time is of the utmost importance."

Derrick rose from his cot and followed Jarvis out of the tree house and through the forest.

"Grandpa, something is wrong. It's still dark?"

"Nothing is wrong. We must make our way unseen and use the darkness of the night to our advantage."

Jarvis used his makeshift wand to guide their way. Derrick struggled to keep up with Jarvis. He felt as if eyes watched him which made his skin crawl. "For an old grandpa, you have some pep in your step."

"It's called staying in shape and not becoming a couch potato."

"Hey, I use my hoverboard."

"Okay, a hoverboard potato. You don't get exercise by riding on that thing. That is what your feet are designed to do, walk and not ride."

"For years, we walked, boat or ride horses to get around the villages but once we were introduce to a new way to travel most folks chose to fly. "I'm not saying it's bad, but it just made us lazy. Now you mentioned a hoverboard. I bet you don't know how to use a broom anymore? Am I right grandson?"

"You're right."

"Explain to me a broom."

"I just looked at it to clean the home and old fashion way to travel. How much further grandpa?" "That's a good start but folks really took proud in their brooms and you should too. Where almost there."

Derrick maintained a close distance to his grandpa so he wouldn't get lost; or worse, eaten by some large creature. They eventually came to a large open field. Jarvis handed Derrick an empty water sack.

"Grandpa, it's empty."

"Then go fill it."

"I don't see a stream."

"It's on the other side of the field."

"Just what I needed, more walking."

"Only if you want to quench your thirsty dusty dry, cracked throat."

"I get it, Grandpa. I'll fetch the water."

As Derrick walked toward the stream, Jarvis changed the field's appearance. The ground split open creating a broad canyon. Derrick froze in his tracks almost stepping off into the abyss. He looked downward; his jaw dropped. He quickly stepped back as his throat closed; his heart thrummed against his ribs. "You could have killed me. How do you want me to cross this, Grandpa? I don't have my wand or board."

"Well now, let me try to figure this out for you; or, are you smart enough to figure it out on your own?"

"I'll take your help."

"Help then it is. You'll do it grandma style and go back to basics." He flicked his hand.

A broom appeared in Derrick's hand as he felt his blood rush through his veins. Sweat beaded across his forehead and upper lip. "Well, it beats hoofing it."

"Did you say hoofing it?" Grandpa flicked his hand, and Derrick's feet turned into hoofs.

"Not funny. Please give me my feet back."

"As you wish." With a flick of his hand, his grandson's feet returned.

"Seriously Grandpa. Now I know all those stories my grandma told me about you are true."

"Get on the broom and fetch us some water."

Derrick blew air from his mouth. "I'm on it." He sat on the broom and tried to recite the spell to fly, but his words mumbled. As he flew, the broom spun out of control which sent him crashing toward the canyon's floor. His life flashed before his eyes. "Grandpa! Grandpa!" His words echoed in the canyon.

"One, two and three." Jarvis waved his wand; the valley returned to the field quickly as Derrick hit the ground with a thud.

"That wasn't funny Grandpa."

"Who said I was trying to be funny. We have a serious war to win. This was just the beginning of your training."

"I don't understand. We've been training for weeks."

"No, I've been getting you into shape for weeks. Now get up and let's get on with the next training exercise."

"Seriously!"

"What part of getting up do you not understand?"

"I get it. I'm up." Derrick stood dusting himself off and immediately grabbed his shoulder. "Ouch! I hurt myself because of your antics."

Grandpa cleared his throat and darted an ice-cold stare toward Derrick.

"Never mind, I'm good." Derrick ignored his shoulder pain. "Bring it on, Grandpa."

A slow grin crisscrossed his grandpa's lips. *By George, he's a Royal after all*. "Are you sure you're ready; what about the water?"

"No time to waste; let's do this."

Two vines wrapped around Derrick's legs and quickly drug him over a rock, the grass and the bushes eventually stopping as he hung over a giant Venus flytrap with its mouth open ready to devour him whole. "Grandpa! Now what?"

"You're on your own with this one; figure it out!"

Derrick took a deep breath. "I need a spell. What freaking spell do I need? The Catapult? The Boomerang? The Whip? The Horse Collar? Invisibility Cloak? Noooo!" His words reverberated throughout the field. He couldn't focus to recall the exact spell he needed to escape the deadly mouth of this large plant. "Turn into a very tiny frog!" He tightened his eyelids. "I'm going to die."

Chomp! Crunch!

Slam! Bash! Thud! The last sounds Derrick heard before the beast devoured him completely; his heartbeat pounded.

"Grandpa!" When he cried out, he remembered his grandpa's sage advice during training. *You sometimes have to look around your surroundings to find your answer.* Right at the last second, he saw a stick inside the beast's stomach and pried its mouth open. He slipped out and crawled away from the plant to a nearby tree. *Grandpa knows some stuff.*

Jarvis gazed proudly upon his grandson. "You survived the ordeal, but I'm disappointed. Why didn't you use the Venus Flytrap spell to escape?"

"You mean there is a spell for this?"

"Need I say more?"

"Seriously Grandpa, you're going to get me killed." Derrick stood brushing the bile juice away from his clothes.

"Not now, Derrick. We have more to achieve today." Jarvis walked over to an old tree stump which stretched over a pond filled with mud. He made two bo staffs appear in his hands. He tossed one to Derrick. "Derrick step onto the old tree stump. It's time to see your hand to hand combat that your grandma taught you."

"You're a trip, Grandpa." Derrick barely lifted the bo staff to defend himself. His energy soon zapped, his shoulder still painful.

"You're going to have to do better than that."

"I'm trying." Derrick's stomach churned with hunger pains.

Jarvis jabbed his staff toward Derrick who avoided Jarvis' attack for a little while before Jarvis's blow swept him off the stump. Derrick tumbled hitting his head and landed in a mud puddle.

"You're young. You can't let an old grandpa like me take you down. Give me ten pushups."

Derrick struggled with the pushups and collapsed face down when he finished the tenth one. "I'm glad that's over."

"Not; give me twenty."

Derrick struggled to complete twenty additional pushups.

"I bet you wish you had that water now."

"I'll gladly go fetch it."

"Not until you move those twenty rocks from one side of the field to the other."

"You've got to be kidding me."

"Of course, I was. I meant to tell you thirty rocks and when you finish that, jog back to camp with a bag full of logs on your back."

Day after day, Jarvis issued impossible tasks for Derrick to complete including repeated the challenges until he could do them faster than anyone did in training before him.

Derrick managed the onslaught of wizard drills his Grandpa Jarvis had placed in his path with remarkable success. After two months of training, Jarvis faced Derrick. "You're ready to face Samuel." He handed him a gift.

Derrick's eyes widened at the sight of his new wand which rested in his palm. He hugged Jarvis. "Grandpa, thank you. I'll use it wisely."

"You earned it. With your magic stronger, we should be able to escape Avalon. Hold my hand and lift your wand into the air."

Derrick nodded as he lifted his wand as he grabbed his grandpa's hand with the other. His eyes darted toward his grandpa's. "The day turns to night; the sun rises in front of thy, transport us to Seven Moon Village which we long to be."

The moons lined up one by one, all seven of them. Derrick marveled at the sight above him. The ground beneath their feet rumbled and shook.

"Grandpa, what's going on?"

"You'll be okay, trust in me, Derrick. Now close your eyes and don't open them until I tell you to."

Derrick closed his eyes.

"You can open them now."

When Derrick opened his eyes, they stood in the middle of the demolished Seven Moon Village. His eyes gazed upward.

"I've never seen the sky this dark, or a salmon-colored moon up. What has happened here?"

"It looks like Samuel's army has destroyed our village."

"Everything I once knew is gone, and this is all my fault."

"You can't blame yourself for this. Help me search and see if we can find anyone still alive."

Jarvis and Derrick searched the area for any survivors or family left by the aftermath of Samuel.

"Grandpa! Over here." Derrick kneeled by a young teenage boy. "What happened here?"

"The dark werewolves came from everywhere. We were overpowered and outnumbered. Your mom and dad fought hard, but Samuel and his troops were too much for them. They took your family and others as slaves, and the dark werewolves killed the rest of the folks in town or turned them into werewolves."

Derrick found two brooms lying on the ground by two dead patrol members; he handed one broom to Jarvis then took off toward Sand Brook Wizard Academy.

While in the sky, Jarvis glowered in disbelief at the destruction of land and trees.

"Derrick don't lose hope. You're the only one who can defeat Samuel."

"I'm going to rescue my family."

"We will, but do you see that dark pinkish moon? It's going to be hard to defeat Samuel. That moon gives him his strength."

"Isn't there a pink moon spell or something?"

"Afraid not. Our best bet right now is to capture one of Samuel's dark werewolf and make him talk."

"There are thousands of them. Look down they are taking over Sand Brook Wizard Academy."

"Follow me, and I'll find us a safe place to land without anyone detecting us."

With one quick swoop, Jarvis snatched one of the dark werewolves and cast a spell of confinement. They landed near a cave and entered dragging the dark werewolf with them.

Jarvis stood over the lackey. “Where is Samuel keeping the prisoners?”

“Where are they keeping my mom and dad?”

“Nothing you two can do will make me defy my master or give you the information you seek.”

Derrick stepped forward. “Watch this grandpa. I learned a thing or two from my dad.” He raised his wand and circled it into the air. “Wiggly, wiggly, piggly poo, watch a slug and watch what it can do.” A truth slug appeared on the tip of Derrick’s wand.

“Nice trick Derrick.” Jarvis nodded in approval.

Derrick placed the truth slug into the lackey’s ear. “This would have been so much easier on you had you just talked. Now where are the prisoners and where are they holding my mom and dad?”

“They have them in the containment bunker a half mile from the academy and are being guarded by four dark werewolves.”

“Well done Derrick. I have a plan to release them.”

“What do we do with him?”

With a flick of his hand, Jarvis turned the lackey into a toad. “Nice look it gives you.”

“Ribbit!”

Derrick remembered the ingredients he needed to create invisible potion, so he searched the area to collect the items he needed. “Okay got it, one spider web, two blue toad mushrooms, an eye of newt and a cup of water.” He crushed them up and then poured the contents on both of them. Their bodies slowly turn invisible.

“Good job Derrick.” “Thanks”

They made their way to the bunker and one at a time eliminated the dark werewolves. Derrick bolted into the bunker to search for his family. Finally, he saw them in a cell at the end. “Mom! Dad!” Kayla and Jacob looked confused not seeing a thing but hearing their names called.

Jarvis entered the area. “Anyone want to be freed?” With the flick of his hand, he lifted the confinement spell.

The doors to the cells open. The invisible potion wore off revealing Derrick standing in front of them.

Kayla rushed toward her son. “Derrick, you’re alive.”

“Son, How did you escape Avalon? How did you find us?”

“I had a little help from a great wizard.”

“Merlin?”

“Grandpa Jarvis. He has been stuck on Avalon Island for years now, all thanks to Samuel.”

Kayla bolted to Jarvis and hugged him.

“Jarvis, I’m so glad you’re alive.” Jacob shook his hand.

“Derrick, have you seen your grandma?”

“She went to look for you the night before you went to Sand Brook Wizard Academy, said Atlas.”

“Son it’s good to see you. Have you seen Atlas?”

“What? No, I haven’t seen either of them in a while. The last time I saw grandma was the night before I left for Sand Brook. I hope she’s okay. The last time I saw Atlas was when I petted him before I went to Sand Brook Wizard Academy.”

Jarvis lifted his brow. “Sabrina has been through some tight situations in her life and knowing that Silver is by her side assures me that she will survive the ordeal.”

“Well Grandpa, how are we going to defeat Samuel and his forces?” Derrick took a deep breath.

Kayla lifted her finger toward Derrick. “I don’t know about you, but I’m not going to let you go out there without us by your side.”

Derrick darted his eyes between his mother and his father as he grinned. *This is the first time in my life that I don’t feel alone. My family has my back; that makes me proud.*

Jacob walked over to them, kneeled and proceeded to draw a diagram of Sand Brook Wizard Academy. He pointed to every entry into the academy. “I think this one is the best way in. It’s the hidden escape hatch used only for the Royal family or Royal Council.”

They all nodded in agreement and then hustled to the escape hatch and traveled through the tunnels beneath the castle. After several minutes, the four prepared for battle. With their wands in their hands, they charged Samuel and

Uriah in the courtyard of the Academy, along with the fighting patrol members and the Royal Patrol members.

Charles snarling stood in front of Derrick. If looks alone could kill, Derrick's life would end at that moment.

Derrick snarled back in return. "I bet you thought you wouldn't see me again after the both of you played me and had me banished."

"Yeah, I did, but I can finish you off by myself."

"You know, I want to thank you for getting me sent there. It opened my eyes to who my real friends are and got me focused on my powers. So, thank you."

Charles morphed into a black grizzly bear. His massive frame tower over Derrick. "Roar" *Oh, wow, he's huge.* He swiped at him with his sharp claws slicing the middle of his shirt. Derrick leaped back to search his body for any wounds.

Charles attacked, but Derrick dodged him. He avoided some of Charles's attacks then struck him with the new skills he learned from his grandpa. Charles collapsed in front of him.

"Too bad Charles. I have only just begun." Derrick waved his wand which sent Charles crashing into the wall. A flick of his wrist created chains around Charles' wrists and ankles. "Let that be a lesson to you. Now I have a bigger battle to fight and a war to win." Derrick made his way to the battle where Jarvis fought head to head with Samuel and Uriah. "I've got this Grandpa. I'm here to help."

Samuel readied his stance. "So, you sent a child to do your dirty work."

"Derrick is no child, but one day he'll be a great wizard. I'm training him."

Samuel and Uriah came at them stronger than Derrick expected, moving earth, and hurling parts of the Academy at them using their magic. He did all he could to avoid the onslaught of attacks they brought to the table.

Jarvis created a wall using stones from the floor to shield them while Derrick shot a big ball of fire directly toward them. They blocked that with a powerful shield created by Samuel. Uriah quickly shot back with a stone from Jarvis's wall. It would have knocked Derrick out if it hadn't been for his mom taking most of the hits.

Derrick leaped onto his feet and returned to the fight just in the nick of time to aid Jarvis holding off the potent powers of Samuel and Uriah.

Samuel flipped open the *Red Wizard Book* to a page toward the back of the book. "Ground below me, the sky above, shake the earth below our feet." The ground began to glow bright yellow. The ground shook like an earthquake. Suddenly, a giant two-headed reticulated python appeared from the field.

Derrick overwhelmed at the size of the beast felt his heart pound against his ribcage. *I can do this. If my family can stand their ground, I can stand mind.* He quickly grabbed his notepad, ripped off one of the pages with a green dragon on it, crumbled it up, and lit it on fire. "With the breath of a dragon and the fire from a stick, turn into a dragon and make it quick."

A green dragon appeared right in front of him. Derrick and Jarvis climbed onto its back. "Dragon attack that ugly python."

The two monsters slammed through most of the structures in the Academy sending dust and stones into the air.

Samuel's powers grew weak as he collapsed across his python.

Derrick and Jarvis targeted Uriah.

So, Uriah used his dark werewolves to attack while he and Samuel escaped on the back of the python into the giant hole. The last of the dark werewolves retreated to the forest, and Derrick stood, proud, with his head up.

When the dust cleared, bodies plastered the area. With his family standing behind him, Derrick realized he could do anything.

Five minutes later, a group of Royal Patrol members surrounded Jarvis and Derrick.

Royal Patrol Member Four nodded in respect toward Jarvis. "The Royal Family would like to see you both immediately, Sir!"

Kayla stepped forward. "If they're going, we're going. I just got him back."

Jacob nodded in agreement. "We're a family and the Blackwell family sticks together."

"Thanks, Mom and Dad."

The Royal Patrol members escorted the Blackwell family to Wisdom hall within minutes. Derrick felt his throat close. His last meeting with the Royal Council didn't work out in his favor. His grandpa patted him on the back and gave him a smile that comforted him. They stood in Wisdom Hall and waited for the King and Queen to speak.

King Damarco sat proudly on his throne; Queen Gabriella at his side with Merlin his adviser stood on the other side. "Silence, everyone. Jarvis, is that you? Where have you been all these years?"

"Yes, it's me. I have been trapped on Avalon Island. Samuel's lackeys trapped me there years ago. I finally escaped that rat-infested place with the help of my grandson, Derrick. Have we been brought here to rehash old times or what?"

"It's good to see you're alive, old friend. I brought you here to regroup and plan our next move. This battle was just a test to see how strong we are now."

"I'm not sure about that, my King, but if that moon turns red, we won't be able to defeat him. Our fate will have been written by then."

"I have already sent a group of some of my best men to track Samuel."

Derrick stepped forward and bowed. "I want to help with this matter, to prove my loyalty to you and as a way to say I'm sorry."

Merlin raised his hand. "We don't need your help. You were supposed to still be on Avalon Island; we are questioning if we should return you there."

"He's my grandson, and I've trained him in our ways. I've seen the growth in him, and I believe he's the only one who can defeat Samuel. I'm willing to vouch for him personally and will take him under my wing, King Damarco! Plus, Derrick just helped us to win this battle."

"I trust you know what you're doing." Merlin looked toward the King.

"Okay you do that, but we still are going to keep an eye on you, Derrick. Guard, please escort Derrick outside the chamber. I need a private word with Jarvis, Kayla, and Jacob."

The guards escorted Derrick out of the hall. He watched the door close. "Nothing to see or do hear guys. I'm going to my dorm room. Bye." Derrick bolted from the area.

The King motioned his hand toward the couch and chairs. "Please, everyone be seated."

Kayla and Jarvis sat on the couch; however, Jacob chose to remain standing.

King Damarco took a deep breath and stared at Jarvis. "We're glad to see you're safe, Dad. As your son-in-law, I feel I can speak for your daughter the Queen as well." He turned his gaze toward Kayla and Jacob. "The Queen and I want to express our gratitude for taking care of Derrick all these years, keeping him safe, and not telling him about us."

Queen Gabriella flashed a small grin. "Here, give Derrick back this compass to protect him." She handed Jarvis the compass as her tears streamed. "And watch over my baby."

"As the King, I have a special favor to ask of Kayla and Jacob. Will you both retrieve my Moon Slayers and to meet up with Jarvis in a day?"

Kayla and Jacob nodded in agreement. She smiled. "It would be our honor, my King."

"One more thing where is Sabrina?" "I'm not sure my Lord, she has disappeared weeks ago. She hasn't returned yet." "Has anybody gone to look for her?" "No" "Well do so."

16. Un-Friendship

Moments in front of the King and Queen felt strange to Derrick; he didn't understand why. As Derrick walked out of Wisdom Hall, a teary-eyed Reign confronted him. She slapped him across his cheek and then hugged him right away. "I'm so angry at you for what you did to get banished but delighted you made it back alive. How could you do this to our village, Derrick?"

"I'm sorry, I didn't think this would get so heinous for all of us."

"Well, when I heard you helped set Samuel free, I couldn't believe my ears."

"I wasn't trying to help Samuel, I wanted to join a group called the Dark Society. I'm not proud of myself, but it is what it is, and all I can do now is to move forward."

"I found out what some clues meant that you gave me a while ago."

"Okay,"

"I think your family was part of the Moon Slayers that Royal Council created years ago. They wanted Royal Patrol members who were strong, brave, smart, and loyal to be assassins and to protect them. Plus, they're supposed to have been disbanded years ago."

"Okay, what are they protecting? And, why are they still in use?"

"Not sure, that's all my friend could find on that. Maybe you need to ask your grandpa more questions about who you are."

Jarvis strode up to Derrick. "Grandson, who his lovely friend who stands next to you?"

"This is Reign Hungry. She is a good friend and student studying to become a witch like Grandma."

"It's nice to meet you, Mr. Blackwell Senior."

"No, no, call me Jarvis."

"Okay, Jarvis. I read a lot about you in my textbooks of what people think happened during the Dark Wars. It's an honor of mine to meet you."

"Thank you, young lady. I think my grandson told me a lot about you, or do I mean a little about you?"

Derrick embarrassed wanted to crawl into the nearest hole.

Jarvis took note of Derrick's behavior and quickly switched to a new subject. "Here Derrick, a gift from me to you."

"Oh, thanks, Grandpa! My compass. You got it back for me."

"It comes with conditions. You must never abuse the power it holds. Understood?"

"Completely."

"Are you ready to head out on our next adventure?"

"Is it okay for Reign to tag along? She could come in handy down the road. This girl has some magic skills."

"Fair enough. Grab items you might need for the trip and meet us at the front gate in five minutes."

"Yes, sir." Reign ran off towards her dorm room.

"Thanks, Grandpa."

"When things get rough, and out of hand, you might not be thanking me then."

"She'll handle anything thrown her way. Grandpa, what are Moon Slayers? Are they real?"

"Wherever did you hear that name?"

"The *Red Wizard Book*."

"I doubt that. Don't say those words again."

What is he hiding? Derrick pursed his lips.

17. Escape from the Darkness

Meanwhile back in Barrett's lair, Sabrina sat in her cage on the ground wearing tattered clothes and stinking from not bathing in weeks. She looked as if half-dead from the daily beatings; her body frail and thin from no food or water grew weak. Her hands clasped by a pair of chains which effectively restricted her magic throbbed.

Separated from her pet Static wolf, Silver, the only thing which kept Sabrina alive was to know that Silver dug to find a way out of his cage ever since confinement in this wretched place. As Sabrina leaned against the bars of her cell, she noticed Silver's head pop out of the ground next to his cell, then went back in after hearing someone walking down the hall toward them.

It was a hairy troll with twenty teeth and one missing eye pushing a cart of food. He opened the bottom door of her cell and slid a plate of slop inside it. Sabrina crawled over to the plate and lifted it to her mouth devouring the slop within minutes.

The hairy troll smirked at Sabrina. "Good doggy, good. I hope you like the leftovers from my master's pets."

Sabrina lifted her head knowing that if she didn't have those chains on, she would rip him a new one. "Silver, come."

Silver managed to squeeze his body through the hole he dug. He walked toward the hairy troll growling. The troll froze, and then slowly turned to see who was behind him. Silver lunged forward sending the troll backward into the bars of the cell that caged Sabrina. She quickly dropped the plate and slid her chains around the troll's neck. "Well, well, well, it seems like the tables have turned now. Hmmm? If you would be so gracious to unlock my right hand with the keys, you have attached to your belt, I might not kill you."

The troll unhooked the keys and handed them to Sabrina. "Now where's my wand and how do we get out of here? Oh yeah, where is my grandson?"

"I'm not telling you anything!" Slobber and snot poured from the troll's mouth and nose.

She tightened her chains around his throat.

"You can do your worst to me. I will never tell you anything." The hairy troll wheezed.

Sabrina squeezed tighter and tighter.

"Okay, okay."

"Here, use my map to guide you through the cave. Derrick's not here anymore. They let him go. Your wand is in Lord Uriah's room."

"Where is Uriah now?"

"With Lord Samuel."

"What? Samuel has been set free?"

"Yes, now let me go."

Sabrina knew he would call for help if she let him go, so she tightened the chains until he lost oxygen and fell unconscious. Sabrina released her grip. "Silver, excellent job." She unlocked her chains and her cell's door. She dragged the troll into her cell and locked him inside. After being in that place for so long, she lost track of time and weeks. She placed Silver in the bottom of the troll's cart and proceeded to use the map to guide her way to Uriah's room.

18. Confusion

Hours after collapsing the tunnel that Samuel's python created, Barrett helped carry Samuel to his carriage and then made the python disappear. Once they took their seats, the door closed, and the driver proceeded to set the carriage in motion. Barrett sat angry, disappointed, and wanting to kill something. He screamed at the top of his lungs. A loud bam! And, another a loud bam from the back of the carriage. He slammed his fist up against the siding.

"Barrett, be quiet! I've heard enough from you. I need to think on my next move."

"But Master, we need to go back now and finish destroying Sand Brook before they can regroup."

"You don't think I know that? But with me not fully healed how far do you think we can get? Not far at all! So if you think you can do it without me, you will fall right onto your face, Grandson. But I can tell you one thing. We will win the next major encounter. Now, pour me a drink."

Barrett reached down to grip the wine bottle from the hidden mini-bar. When Samuel looked away, Barrett added a few drops of his X potion into Samuel's wine and then handed it to him.

He watched as Samuel consumed his wine, and then he gave him another.

"Is the Scarlet Witch waiting for us to arrive at Waldorf Wizard Academy?"

"Yes Grandpa, I have sent a lackey ahead to let her know we're coming." *I hope this potion the Scarlet Witch gave me restricts his power.*

Samuel's eyes became heavy, and he fell asleep.

***

Back at Sand Brook Wizard Academy, Derrick and Jarvis sat upon two horses alongside a mounted group of Royal Patrol members waiting for Reign to arrive with her bag for the trip. Jarvis pulled out his pocket watch to see the time. "I'm afraid Derrick, your friend is a no show. There is no sign of her. Royal Patrol, let's move out."

Derrick tugged on his horse's reins and gently kicked the beast's side.

"Wait! Wait! I'm sorry I'm late. I couldn't find a few things."

"Grandpa, I told you she'd make it."

"Just in the nick of time."

Derrick watched Reign galloped up to them on her horse. A small grin appeared as he tried not to stare at her. *Is she galloping in slow motion?*

"We were about to leave, but I'm glad you made it young lady? Now, let's get moving."

The group approached the dark forest as Jarvis's hawk, Sky, motioned for them to head toward it. Three hours of riding brought them to the perfect resting point. Jarvis dismounted his horse. "We'll make camp here and rest. At sunrise, we will continue our journey."

Everyone dismounted their horses and immediately went to work setting up camp.

Derrick retrieved wood from the forest to start a bonfire. He wanted to practice doing an exercise that Jarvis showed him at Avalon Island. Derrick placed his wand on the ground and sat with his legs crossed. He closed his eyes and breathed in and out, in and out. It felt like five minutes went past as Derrick as nothing happened to the branches. Beads of sweat formed across his forehead as he opened one eye. "What! Nothing is happening."

Jarvis exhaled. "Relax Derrick and concentrate on the task at hand."

Derrick shook off whatever troubled him; the branch caught on fire and grew bigger and bigger.

"Great! Great, Derrick! Now absorb it and send it back with dragon breath." With a sharp blow, he sent the flame toward the sky.

Jarvis patted Derrick on his back.

"I'm proud of you, grandson."

"Thanks, Grandpa. I'm kinda of proud of you as well."

Reign giggled. "I'm proud to know both of you." She yawned and stretched. "I'm calling it a night, it's been a long day, and it will be a longer day tomorrow."

Jarvis grinned. "You're a smart young lady. I think everyone needs to sleep."

The group dispersed to their sleeping area they created with leaves and the blanket from their saddles.

Derrick fell to sleep quickly, but he soon tossed and turned. Within minutes his troubled sleep worsened. "No! No! I have to save Grandma."

Reign leaned over him and shook him.

"Hold on, Derrick. It's me, Reign. You were thrashing around in your sleep."

Derrick opened his eyes and looked up at Reign in a daze.

"Are you okay?"

"I'm not sure. I had a nightmare about my grandma."

"What was it about?"

"My Grandma Sabrina was locked in a cage on the brink of death and chained to a wall. Fifty percent of her body was covered in wounds and scars. I felt her turmoil and pain. Then Uriah came from the shadows and cut her neck. I tried to save her."

"Do you realize that was only a dream?"

"I think I do, but it seemed so real to me."

"Try not to think about it anymore. I've been thinking about the clues again."

"What about them?"

"Something doesn't add up for me when it comes to the clues you gave me. We figured out that your parents were a part of some Moon slayer group, Mr. Bishop was a spy, and Charles used you to retrieve items to bring back to Uriah. Are we missing anything else?"

"Yeah, Barrett broke my wand, and I received a compass that only works for royalty and my teddy bear."

"What was the reason for Barrett breaking your wand?"

"Maybe he wanted to make me mad and humiliate me."

"No, he could do that any other day. I think Barrett is working with Uriah too."

"What does he have to gain from the situation?"

"Don't you remember? Barrett is related to Samuel."

"Oh yeah, I forgot that. Okay, what about my compass? I'm not royalty."

"You don't look like your parents that much if you ask me. Maybe your parents are King Damarco and Queen Gabriella, and you're adopted. Ha, ha, ha, just playing, Derrick. Let's get some sleep before we have to get going."

"What's so funny? That makes sense to me now. I always wondered if I was adopted. My mannerisms are different from theirs, and I found baby clothes in the attic years ago with a royal seal on them, but my parents just denied any connection with them."

"Maybe you should ask your grandpa. He seems like a wise and honorable man who would tell you the truth."

"I think I will do that." As Derrick looked over at his grandpa who stood guard near the campsite with a few Royal Patrol members. He stood, dusted himself off and proceeded to walk to Jarvis.

19. Facing the Truth

Sabrina moved to Barrett's room weaving through the maze of tunnels. Once she arrived, Sabrina found her wand stuffed inside a glass case. She grabbed the cart and took off toward the opening of the cave.

The cart's wheels clinked as Sabrina strolled past several guards. One guard stood. "You there. Clean the pit and finish feeding the dark werewolves."

She pulled her hood down lower to cover her face. "Yes sir, I will get on that immediately."

The guard continued his round, and when he turned the corner, she kept moving toward the entrance of the cave. After thirty minutes, Sabrina emerged from the cave covering her eyes because of the brightness barely able to see for ten seconds.

She looked around for guards and only saw eight chatting beneath a tree. When she started toward the forest, one guard stopped her.

"What are you doing up here? You're supposed to be cleaning and feeding Lord Bloodstone's dark werewolves right now."

"I was getting a bit of fresh air and a walk, sir."

"Nobody told you, you could do that. You people don't like fresh air and light."

As he reached out to pull her back, his whole body went numb, and he stood in a trance. Sabrina knew her magic not fully restored would not hold him for long, so she made him do a few commands while she could. "You listen to me. Send the surrounding guards off toward the mountains; then you walk back in that cave. One more thing. Where is Uriah heading to now?"

"To Waldorf Village."

Once Sabrina was far enough into the forest Silver slid out from beneath the cart, she whistled for her horse, climbed on, and took off toward Waldorf Village.

***

After five hours of riding through the woods, Barrett's carriage arrived at Waldorf Village. Barrett's driver stood upon the carriage, held a golden trumpet to his lips, and played an announcement eight-note melody. The tree leaves turned from yellow to red to blue, and then white as they fell to the ground opening the gates to Waldorf Village.

The driver took a seat, snapped the reins, and guided the horses through the gates toward their destination.

***

Back at the campsite, Derrick stood next to Jarvis. "Hey, Grandpa, can I speak to you?"

"Sure, what do you need, Derrick?"

"Will you promise a wizard's promise that can't be broken and tell me the truth and not lie to me?"

"Okay, I thought this time would come. I just didn't expect here or now. You have my wizard's promise."

Derrick took a deep breath. "Where do I start? Are you my real grandpa? Is Grandma my grandma? Who are my real parents, and why did the Royal Family allow me to come away with you and not send me back to the island?"

"That was a mouthful. Where do I start? Your grandma and I are your real grandparents. Your birth parents are King Damarco and Queen Gabriella. They sent you away years ago as a baby to Kayla and Jacob for your protection. They didn't want to, but because they loved you, they had to because Samuel planned to kill you. Your parents decided to have your Grandma Sabrina and me, plus two Royal Patrol members protect you over these years. They wanted to give you a normal life, so they placed you with us. You're the future ruler of Seven Moon."

"I thought King Damarco and Queen Gabriella lost their son giving birth to him years ago. Why didn't they tell me? Why did they send me away like that to a scary place like Avalon?"

"They wanted to tell you, but after your last betrayal, King Damarco sent you away to Avalon hoping you would learn from your mistakes. Plus, your adopted parents, Sabrina, and I were placed under oath not to tell you until you were old enough to know the truth."

"So why are you telling me this now?"

"I made a wizard promise to you. Besides that, I feel guilty about not telling you when we first met on the island. I hope you can forgive all of us one day."

"I don't know right now! You just gave me a ton of information that makes me question everything you people ever told me. What else have you not told me?"

"For right now, that's all the information I'm willing to give. Now, try to get some sleep. We will be leaving soon."

"No! I think I will take a walk to clear my conscience." *Reign was right, I am royalty. Wait! That makes me a prince. Take that Barrett!*

"Take a Royal Patrol member along with you."

Derrick walked off.

Jarvis waved at a Royal Guard. "Follow him."

"Sir, I don't see him."

Jarvis jerked his head one way and then to the other looking for Derrick. "Derrick! Where are you, Grandson? Royal Patrol members, find me my Grandson now!"

While Derrick ran through the forest, he heard a noise coming from behind. He stopped in his tracks. "Show yourself."

Reign stepped from the shadows. "Hey! Why are you acting like a five-year-old right now? This is not the time for that attitude."

"I don't know who to trust anymore. I just found out my world has been a lie, and I don't know if I'm willing to deal with the secrets."

"You can trust me!" Reign touched Derrick's hand while looking into his eyes. The whole mood changed at that moment between Derrick and Reign. He went in for a kiss but stopped when Royal Patrol Member Fifteen came out from the bushes.

"Ah! There you are, Derrick. We've been looking for you everywhere. Your grandpa has been worried about you. He wants you to come back to the campsite. Do you have any problem with that?"

"No! We can go back to the campsite."

"Prince, here take my horse back to the campsite. I can walk back."

Reign's brow creased. "Did he just address you as Prince? As in royalty, Prince?"

Derrick nodded as he hopped onto the back of the horse. "Climb aboard my fair maiden." He extended his hand for Reign to ride along with him. She got on, and they rode back to camp. "I guess the cat is out of the bag. You were right. I am a Prince."

"Details. I want all the juicy details."

"Let me wrap my head around this, okay?"

"Whatever you need, my Prince."

"Stop calling me that."

***

As Kayla flew on her broom, she noticed the moon turned a deep pink, so she hurried to meet with Jarvis. Kayla, along with twenty Moon Slayers, landed near Jarvis's campsite. She identified herself by holding up her ancient stone with the Royal Crest stamped on it, and a secret handshake.

Jarvis walked over and embraced his old friends. "I'm glad you arrived on time."

"I had to scour the hillsides, farms, outskirts of the villages to find these Moon Slayers."

"Job well done. Kayla and Jacob, I told Derrick who is real parents are."

Kayla's smile evaporated. "You had no right. That was our place."

"I didn't have much choice. The boy is smart. He figured it out and confronted me."

Jacob cleared his throat. "How did he take it?"

"Not that well. He'll wrap his head around it in time. I have full faith and confidence. Look, here he comes now."

Royal Patrol Member Fifteen helped Reign and Derrick off the horse.

Instead of greeting his parents, Derrick just walked over to his stuff, placed everything in his bag, and then secured it to his horse. He climbed back up on his horse and waited for his Grandpa to give the signal to leave.

Jarvis approached him. "Hold on right there, young man; your parents don't deserve your attitude."

"They're not my real parents, Grandpa! Why should I listen to them?"

"They might not be your biological parents, but they raised you like their own."

"Not really! I spent most of my childhood with Grandma. She is more like a parenting figure than these two."

A tear fell down Kayla's cheek. "Derrick's right about us. We were thrown into all of this by King Damarco and weren't ready to care for a child."

Jacob flashed a thin-lipped grin toward Derrick. "Son, we messed up! All of us involved. We should have had a conversation with you years ago, but we were bound by the King and Queen to keep this a secret so the Dark Society wouldn't find you."

Kayla wiped her tears. "We love you son. You see, Derrick, the night that you were born Samuel was planning to kill you so you couldn't stop him from being the ruler of the world. When we learned about it, we did everything we could to keep you safe."

"So why didn't the King and Queen come to get me? Don't they love me?"

"Yes! They truly do, and we do too Derrick. Plus they didn't know who to trust around the academy." Kayla sniffled.

Derrick huffed. "So this is the reason you both were always gone? You're Moon Slayers?"

"What? How do you know we're a part of that group?"

"I was in your lab the other night snooping around and saw the Dark Werewolf in the cage. Sorry, Dad."

"I knew I was right about that. But yes, we have been doing dangerous missions for the Royal Council. Top secret stuff, son, we're sorry too, about all of this, Derrick."

Derrick hugged his family. "I'm sorry for everything. Grandpa, what's our next move?"

Jarvis scratched his cheek. "Kayla, have you located the whereabouts of Sabrina?"

"No, it's like she fell off the world. Nobody can find her anywhere Jarvis, but we will find her soon."

"Don't worry about Sabrina. She can handle herself. She's a tough person. She'll turn up soon, I can feel it. Everyone it is time to move out. Mount your horses and brooms. We move in five toward Waldorf Village."

20. I Will Conquer

Two Hours later, Barrett and Samuel arrived at the Waldorf Wizard Academy. "Master, you don't look so great. Your eyes are dark, like really dark."

"I'm fine."

I guess the potion worked. Barrett felt a sense of accomplishment; he beat the Master at his own game.

The door of the carriage flew open. A few lackeys rushed and assisted Samuel who could barely stand to the Scarlet Witch with Barrett at their side.

The academy buzzed from the arrival of Samuel and Barrett. Students stood in doorways and stairwells to get a glimpse as they traveled through it. They arrived at a gray room lit by candles on the third floor. A wooden table with chains attached to it sat in the middle of the room. The lackeys placed Samuel on the Scarlet Witch's table while placing chains upon him.

Samuel turned to Barrett. "What is going on with me, Grandson? I should be fully recovered now. Did you put something in my drink, you rotten, disrespectful child? You're not ready for more power."

"You know, old man, I realized when you were in the Dark Void that I didn't want to be controlled by you anymore. I want the power and the glory of controlling this despicable world. And, with your power matched with mine I can, Grandfather."

The Scarlet Witch about five feet three, light skinned with green eyes wore a black and dark purple dress with a purple silk scarf over her nose and mouth appeared from the shadows. "Welcome to my chambers, Samuel."

"You're not going to get away with this. Neither of you."

"Grandpa, we already have."

The witch placed four green stones around his body and chanted from a large book. "Disesphene. Enehpsesid!" The four green stones lifted from the table as they absorbed the power from Samuel's body.

The green stones merged as one and landed in Barrett's hand. He grinned and then hooked them to his chain around his neck. "Now, let's destroy the army that King Damarco sent after us."

***

Elsewhere, as Jarvis rode closer and closer to Waldorf Wizard Academy, the moon turned light red. Jarvis glanced toward it. *Derrick is the only one who can defeat Samuel now.* "Derrick, place the compass around your neck. You must wear it at all times. It will protect you."

As Derrick and the others rode through Waldorf Village, they noticed the streets were vacant. Not a soul in sight. "Grandpa, I have a bad feeling about this."

"Channel your thoughts on protection."

Kayla glanced downward toward Jacob. "Protect him with your life. I must go with the Moon Slayers."

"You don't have to tell me."

Jarvis looked at Jacob. "Jacob, I need you to be on your toes in this battle it's going to be ugly, and I know you have the skills and tools to handle the wounded."

"Okay sir, I'm on it."

Suddenly, the ground turned to quicksand, swallowing those who were on horses up to their necks. Barrett stood on the overlook of Waldorf Wizard Academy smirking from ear to ear.

Kayla fought hard to stick to the plan after seeing Derrick get stuck in quicksand, but she knew Jarvis and Jacob wouldn't let anything happen to her son. So, Kayla, along with the Moon Slayers crept through the woods to surround Waldorf Wizard Academy surrounded by a ton of dark werewolves.

Derrick turned his head toward the sounds of scraping steel and trees splitting coming from the forest. He still couldn't escape from the quicksand hardening around him. "Grandpa, can you escape?"

"I'm working on it."

Jacob stood back. "Remain calm son. Don't move or you'll sink until we can get your out of there."

Barrett raised his hand and launched several energy balls toward Derrick intending to quickly finish this battle before it began.

Sabrina deflected the energy balls away from Derrick. "Hold on Derrick; I'm going to get all of you out of here. Sky above release your grip and release these men from the quicksand tombs."

Once Jarvis got to his feet, he flashed a grin to Sabrina. "What took you so long to show up, Dear?"

"I was held captive for a while, but I'm here now. Did you think that I was going to let you and the rest of my old friends have all the fun?"

"I knew you would show up, eventually. You look beautiful." Jarvis swirled his hands and his clothes instantly changed to clean ones.

"Jarvis, this is neither the time nor place for that. Now, create a fog to get us close to Waldorf Wizard Academy."

Barrett's smile turned to a frown after Sabrina deflected the energy balls and released Derrick from his tomb. He lifted his wand to bring the four concrete ogres to life that resided along the gates of the academy.

"Jarvis, anytime now on that fog." Sabrina narrowed her eyes.

A thick fog flooded the area like a tidal wave of water which confused the ogres. One ogre grabbed Reign while as she passed.

Jarvis bolted toward Jacob.

Jacob and another Royal Patrol Med helped the wounded Patrol and Royal Patrol Members to a safe location to work on them. "Be careful Derrick, make us proud."

"Bye, Dad. I love you." Derrick transformed his wand into a sword and then ran toward the ogre chopping off one of the ogre's legs. The ogre fell to the ground, and he sliced off the ogre's head. Derrick helped Reign to her feet. "Are you okay, Reign?"

"Yeah, I am fine."

"Don't worry about those ogres." Kayla emerged from the fog. "The Moon Slayers and I will handle them. Just destroy the *Red Wizard Book* before the moon turns dark red."

Barrett's face turned beet red. "No! My plan is not going to fail this way." He stared down at the thick fog taking away his vision. He waved his wand creating a strong wind which pushed the fog out of the village. "Where are you, Derrick? You can run, but you can't hide." He stared down at the empty village. "Guards, find him!"

21. The Beast Within

Derrick, Reign, Jarvis, Sabrina and a few Moon Slayers arrived at the Academy's wall from the direction of the lake which flowed around the Academy and along the village. They used the stones from the wall to form stairs to get onto the barely open drawbridge. Once inside the Academy courtyard, the Scarlet Witch's three guards spotted them. "Stop there. You're not allowed to lay foot on this ground. Place your weapons on the ground." The Scarlet Witch's lieutenant alerted the rest of the guards.

"Go, Derrick. We can handle these guys alone." Her tone snapped Derrick into action.

Derrick grabbed Reign's hand, and they bolted toward the academy's room. As they sprinted up four flights, their footsteps echoed throughout the stairwell. When they arrived at the top, they glared upward. "Reign, we're out of time. Look, the moon has turned to dark red."

"It's never over until it's over and it's not over, yet."

"I like the way you think. It's not over."

Barrett placed his mystical mask over his face and used his lackeys as a chair. "Hey Derrick, it's nice to see you again. I've been waiting for you to arrive. Do you honestly think you're just going to come up here with her and defeat me?"

"Actually, yes."

Barrett cracked his knuckles, and then he pushed over his lackeys as he stood up.

Before Uriah could summon his power, Derrick quickly inhaled and raised his index and middle finger to his lips and blew dragon breath at him burning off half Barrett's mask.

Uriah pulled off the other half and laughed. "You know, that mask was getting hot. I guess the jig is up."

Reign's jaw dropped. "Barrett, is that you? You're a despicable, rotten and evil jerk."

Barrett grabbed his face as it transformed into a dark werewolf. His jawline lengthened, and his skin changed from pale to burgundy as his body enlarged and hair rapidly covered it. He used both hands to rip off his shirt. With the help of the red moon, Barrett evolved into a different breed of dark werewolf. He lunged toward Derrick slicing his shirt to shreds, then knocked him through a glass window.

Derrick landed in a room up against a desk. He tried to get up, but Barrett grabbed him by his throat and hurled him through furniture sending him crashing into walls which fractured his ribs. Barrett howled as he stood on the debris while grasping Derrick.

Blood streamed down Derrick's face as Barrett grabbed him by his left ankle and dangled him out the window.

Derrick could hardly breathe because of his broken ribs. He touched his left shoulder which felt as if it dislocated during the fight. To top all of that, his swollen and bruised right eye throbbed. He stared down at the ground below, and the fighting in the courtyard.

Barrett smirked in disgust. "Let's finish this story between us."

Reign jumped onto Barrett's back and raked her fingers through his eyes.

Barrett released Derrick, sending him falling head first.

Derrick latched onto a windowsill and pulled himself inside to a partially darkened room. He crawled toward the door clutching his chest. His hand landed onto a wooden table, and then on a human leg. "I'm not alone; am I?"

"Help me, help me. I'm only a weak old man."

"What side of the battle are you on?"

"Your side, young man."

After Derrick pulled himself to his feet, he used his wand to light the room and gazed upon a wrinkly, white-bearded old man with fancy clothes, chained to the wooden table.

"Who are you, old man, and why are you chained to this table?"

Derrick doesn't know I'm Samuel. Maybe I can use him to help me escape and retrieve my power. "I'm Alexander, a humble servant at the Waldorf Academy. They accused me of stealing something to eat, and now I'm here."

Screams came from above; Derrick's eyes darted in that direction. "Reign! Look, it's only a matter of time before Barrett heads this way. Why should I unchain you, old man?"

"Because I can help you defeat Uriah."

"You mean Barrett?"

"Yeah, yeah him."

"I don't know if I should trust you, old man, so I'm going to leave you right where you are. I'll deal with you later after I deal with Barrett."

"Wait! What would your parents think of you if you just left an old man like me lying here like this?"

Derrick pondered for a second. "Chains, chains unbind this man, let him be free to use his hands." The chains unlocked and fell from the old man. "You better help me, Alexander or I'll end, your life."

Back on the roof in the adjacent room, Barrett rubbed his werewolf eyes with his paw. He jerked Reign off his back with the other and then slapped her sending her hard flying smashing into the door. He tossed decks and beds to the side as he sneered.

Reign stood to her feet. "This isn't over Barrett."

He lunged toward her to stab her into the chest, but she vanished and reappeared behind him smashing a chair onto him which sent him falling forward. She quickly wrapped her cape tightly around Barrett's body and then transformed her wand into a sword. As she swung toward him, he caught the sword with his fangs, and then slammed her hard as he could into the stone wall. He ripped through the cape as he watched the stone wall crash down onto Reign.

Barrett climbed out of the window and scaled the wall looking around for Derrick, but there was no sign of him in the area nor on the ground.

Barrett sniffed trying to pick up Derrick's scent. His nose stopped on Derrick's blood which smeared the windowsill.

Elsewhere in Waldorf Wizard Academy, Derrick struggled to help Alexander through the halls. The walls covered with pictures of deceased faculty and students came to life as they passed.

"Young man, here's a janitor's closet. We can hide in there, and I can tend to your wounds."

"Do you hear that?"

"I believe that would be Barrett heading our way."

Derrick knew his time in hiding was just about up, but he needed to know how to defeat Barrett. He thought before he spoke. "All right, Alexander, how do I get rid of Barrett?"

"You need to get hold of that stone that's on that chain that he has around his neck; that will decrease his power."

Before Alexander could say anything else, Barrett came crashing through the wall behind them. Derrick immediately let go of Alexander, then reached in his jacket for his deck of cards and used his power to send them darting toward Barrett's chain. Soon, the chain around Barrett's neck broke as the stone fell to the ground. Derrick grabbed a sword mounted in the hall, leaped in the air, slashed off Barrett's left arm, and then pushed him over a railing.

"Ha, ha. Did you think doing this would kill me, Derrick?" Barrett picked up his arm and reattached it. "I can regenerate under a dark red moon."

Derrick reached down to retrieve the chain, then turned to grab Alexander to high tail it out of there. On the way down the hall, Derrick handed Alexander the chain. "Now, Alexander, what do we do?"

Samuel lifted the chain with the stone to his teeth, ripped it from the chain, and then swallow it. His power and youth returned. As Derrick held Samuel, he placed Derrick in a trance sealing spell with his right hand. *Once a reality, is now a dream, wrap the Rings Amber round his wrist and seal whom I touch in thee.*

"You tricked me. I knew I shouldn't have helped you."

"You're not wise enough young warlock."

Derrick's eyes felt heavy, and his vision blurred in and out of focus as Samuel's sealing trance spell took effect. He couldn't move as if stuck in concrete. His eyes closed. *Old man, why?*

Barrett returned to the second floor. "I'm going to rip you to shreds Derrick Blackwell and enjoy every minute! Samuel transported himself over towards Barrett, grabbed his throat, and slammed him to the ground as his grandson tried to rip him apart.

"I should kill you grandson right where you stand, but I must say I was impressed how far you would go to achieve what you wanted.

"If you don't get a hold of that transformation of yours, you will be no different from the beast you control or should I say, try to control. Now stand up, dust yourself off, and show me where your grandmother is, Barrett."

He stood up, dusted himself off, and strode down the hall.

"Hey, Grandson, are you forgetting something?"

"What are you talking about, Granddad?"

"Ah, bringing Derrick with us."

"He isn't going anywhere, thanks to your trance. I will get my lackeys to retrieve him for us."

***

Sabrina and Silver had a group of dark werewolves chasing them around the academy. She turned the corner. "Oh my god, Derrick." She quickly used her magic to collapse the wall to the left of her to give her some time to think her next move. "Something is definitely wrong with my grandson there's no time to evaluate. "Silver, give us time to escape boy." Silver nodded his head and prepared for an onslaught of dark werewolves.

The troop of werewolves busted through the debris, headed toward them. "There's no time." Sabrina opened a nearby window, grabbed Derrick, and leaped out. They plunged into the water below which swept them away carried by the powerful current.

Silver fought the werewolves holding them back as long as he could.

The dark werewolves raced over to the open window and witnessed Sabrina struggling to hold her grandson above the water. They leaped out the window and scaled the side of the building, then jumped across the river chasing after them. A floor below Jarvis and Moon Slayer Twelve fought Howling Fang and several guards of Waldorf Wizard Academy. As Jarvis's head turn he witness Sabrina and Derrick falling from the academy. "No, Sabrina and Derrick! They fell in the nearby river. We get to going now." Jarvis raised his wand. "Water that's all around us come together and freeze them where they stand."

Howling Fang and the guards froze in a big block of ice. "They need us; she won't be able to hold him much longer." "Right, sir. Extend your branch to me old tree at a far, allow me to use you as a repelling tool." One big tree branch came crashing through the window.

***

Meanwhile, on the roof, Reign came to, her head spun as she lay trapped beneath the rubble. *I hope Derrick is still alive.*

The sounds of metal and bone echoed through the academy from all the onslaught of the Moon Slayers and dark werewolves fighting.

Derrick, please stay alive. I need you.

***

Sabrina, tired and sore, swallowed a lot of water. *I don't have enough strength or the power to survive this predicament.*

Suddenly, two big splashes hit the water as Sabrina closed her eyes. *Please save my grandson!*

Silver dragged Derrick to the shore as Jarvis rescued Sabrina.

She drifted in and out of consciousness laying on the bank beside the river. "Silver isn't here." Her words faded.

Jarvis revived her while Moon Slayer Twelve and Silver kept the remaining dark werewolves at bay. Silver charged after a pack and followed them into the forest.

Jarvis placed Sabrina and his grandson gently into the back of a wagon.

Moon Slayer Twelve leaped onto the front seat. "Watch your family, I'll take the reins. Where did Silver disappear to?"

Sabrina moaned in pain. "Where's Silver?"

"He is chasing some dark werewolves. He'll catch up with us. Let's go."

Silver howled at the dark red moon surrounded by a pack of dark werewolves led by Howling Fang.

Jarvis took a deep breath and darted his eyes toward Moon Slayer Twelve. "Speaking of chasing werewolves, we haven't seen or heard from Kayla since she took off after them with the Moon Slayers. I hope she's okay."

"Kayla knows what she's doing. Keep the faith."

Sabrina stretched her arm over onto Derrick as if to protect him. *He's dreaming, I can tell.*

***

Derrick walked over to the Red Wizard Book, *closed it, and then used his magic to place it into his back pocket. Derrick reached for Reign's hand, then proceeded to leave the roof. As he opened the door and stepped out of the room, the sun blinded him. He walked through the tall grassy plain, and he witnessed deer grazing while others challenged each other. Sparrows and robins flew around him. "I remember this. It's our sixth-grade class on a field trip."*

"I remember too." Reign smiled at Derrick. "We went through the forest with Ms. Smalls, the biology teacher. She seems different from her typical bubbly personality."

"She seems fine to me."

They made their way over to Fawn, a girl in the class who competed with Reign to be Miss Teacher's pet, played in a field of dwarf wild roses.

Derrick snuck up on her and scared her into a poison ivy bush. He laughed and pointed at Fawn until he noticed she wasn't laughing back.

"Derrick, why did you do that?" Fawn stomped her foot.

"Just chill, I was playing around with you. It was just a bush you fell into."

"That was just a bush? A bush, no, it was poison ivy! I was trying not to fall in it; you dill weed. If you read your biology book all the way through, you would know what that was next to me."

"Oh, sorry for that, Fawn, that wasn't my intention to do that to you."

As he finished his last word, Ms. Smalls gripped him up from behind and dragged him to the carriage that was sitting to the left of him. As Derrick stepped inside the carriage, the area changed. He appeared at his cart which he usually performed at on the streets of Copper Town. It was five o'clock, and the sky was partly cloudy with scattered rain showers. The smog covered brick buildings that surrounded the small park. Copper lanterns lined the cobbled-stone streets throughout town. Derrick now about thirteen had a somewhat slow day to obtain tips from folks who passed on their way home.

He packed his cart as a group of students from one of the local high schools approached him. "Do some magic for us."

He performed a simple card trick, but they didn't like it.

"I have already seen that trick, so do another one, dweeb!"

So, Derrick did.

"Boo! Boo! Boo!" The group pelted him with rocks and fruit until they knocked him out. Then, they stole his money and vandalized his cart.

***

"Okay you sleepyheads, it's time to wake up. We're approaching Copper Town." Jarvis glanced over his shoulder.

Sabrina woke up and shook Derrick. "Wake up. Jarvis, he's not waking up. He needs help. My magic isn't working to wake him. Moon Slayer Twelve, drive us to Copper Town at once. Thank you, Jarvis, for saving us; another second and I would have drowned. I'm apprehensive about Derrick. I think he's having a nightmare. I feel his struggle."

Derrick deep in a trance played out a battle in his trapped mind.

***

Led by Derrick, Jarvis, Sabrina, and Silver headed upstairs to retrieve the Red Wizard Book.

When they entered the room upstairs, Barrett's two lackeys ripped off their shirts. Their bodies enlarged as well as their hair thickened as they transformed into dark werewolves. They stood their ground guarding the Red Wizard book.

I need to use the Clone spell. Derrick reached into his soggy back pocket and grabbed his notepad. "Wetness of water evaporate." All soggy clothes and all wet items instantly dried. Derrick drew a sketch of Silver and then ripped the page out setting it on fire. "Silver, Silver double-time, give me one more of you to be mine." Instantly Sliver's clone appeared standing at Derrick's side. "Silvers, attack."

As the wolfs attacked the two dark werewolves, Derrick lunged for the Red Wizard Book.

Boom! The doors flew open. Barrett smashed into the room sending the furniture flying.

Sabrina used her power to hold back the group of dark werewolves racing toward her.

Derrick's grandparents fought Barrett until he retrieved the Red Wizard Book. His compass glowed as he held the magic book. The compass flipped the pages stopping on a spell. "I can't read this."

Like the voice of God from the heavens, the translation reverberated in Derrick's mind. "Thank you, compass."

Barrett broke free of Jarvis and Sabrina and charged toward Derrick.

"With the power of thy will and thy truest heart, turn each werewolf to stone mid-strife."

Suddenly, Barrett, along with the dark werewolves throughout the land turned into statues in mid-stride.

Jarvis proudly smiled. "You've grown wise these past few days. Now one more spell and we can put this to rest."

"I know the one." Derrick took a deep breath. "Mystical Moon, magical Moon, turn from dark red to the Man on the Moon. White as can be, let me see, all of your purity."

The red dark moon transformed into a brilliant full moon.

"I did it. Reign? I have to find Reign?" He bolted to the rooftop and searched the rubble for any sign of Reign. "Reign!" He moved a large sheet a metal. "Reign! Where are you?" His heart sank as he felt an emptiness in the pit of his stomach.

"Derrick, is that you?"

"Reign, where are you?"

"Over here. You'll have to dig me out."

Derrick sprinted to a pile of rocks. "Don't worry; I'll get you out." Derrick nodded confidently. "Rocks of wall which make me stumble, move thyself back from the rubble."

The rocks rose and assembled back into a wall.

Derrick grabbed Reign's hand. "You okay?"

"I am thanks to you. Where's Barrett?"

"It's over for now." He hugged her. When he let go, he looked at her eyes, and then they passionately kissed.

***

The wagon emerged from the forest and followed the trail for ten minutes. Sabrina stroked Derrick's hair. "I think his nightmare ended, I sensed peace."

Jarvis darted his eyes toward Moon Slayer Twelve. "Let's stop here for a quick stretch."

The wagon came to a stop at the top of a hill.

"Silver! Where are you, Silver?"

"I told you he'd catch up; he's a smart dog. Don't worry about him; he can take care of himself."

Jarvis amazed by the overall advance of the dominant society grinned as he stared down upon Copper Town. The three ways to enter include the main bridge, by train or by boat. The town's lanterns placed throughout and cobblestone streets; blooming trees in pinks, purple and blue, storefronts and several steam-powered cars zooming about seemed advance to Jarvis. "This place has changed since my years spent on Avalon Island, and how the world had changed outside the village."

Sabrina frowned. "It's sad to see our land like this. We don't have time for this if we are going to save Derrick."

"Moon Slayer Twelve, let's go."

The wagon pulled forward and finally arrived at Smith Field Avenue. A young boy stood on the corner selling newspapers. "Extra, extra read all about it."

Sabrina tossed him a few coins and took a paper with the headline – *"Mayor Takes Stand."* She read from the newspaper. "Listen to this everyone. Mayor Bill Goldwin said on Tuesday that Copper Town is experiencing a phenomenon. He's not sure what is going on right now. But, with the recent killings happening around the town, he is putting the town on lockdown and wants all his citizens to stay in their homes if they don't have to venture out. And, now this article, *Wild Beast on the Run.* Last Wednesday, a woman was bitten by a wild dog or man and ended up killing her entire family. The authorities are asking for any information on her whereabouts."

Jarvis shivered. "I don't like the way any of that sounds."

Sabrina tapped Moon Slayer Twelve on the shoulder. "Turn right at Green Burgh Street, and then a left at Walnut Street."

The wagon proceeded through the town until it pulled over between a pet store and a saloon.

Jarvis' brow creased. "Why are we stopping between a pet store and a saloon? Are we getting a pet or a drink?"

"None of those, we have arrived at Kofu's place." Jarvis squinted her eyes. What! Where?"

"Over there in that alley." Sabrina's index finger lifted toward a small gap between the buildings.

"Are you pointing toward that four-inch space?"

Sabrina stepped off the wagon looking around the area before walking up to the gap between the buildings. She clapped her hands. "Gap before me grow and grow to reveal thy true size, make it so."

The gap increased exposing a gorgeous three-story building with three Royal Guards standing post.

Jarvis stepped off the wagon carrying Derrick over his shoulder like a potato sack. As they approached the three royal guards, the one in the middle stepped forward. "Halt! Don't come any further. What is the reason you are in my presence? State it now or die where you stand."

"We're here to see Kofu about important matters. Can't you see this boy is ill?" Sabrina smiled.

"Well, Kofu is not accepting any visitors at the time. So, leave!"

Jarvis stepped forward. "Wait, I'm Agent One, and I was told to report here if I had an emergency. We have permission from the Royal Council. Here is my proof of who I am." Jarvis held his palm toward him. "Now, tell Kofu his old friend, Jarvis is here to see him."

The Royal Guard searched Jarvis' mind with his mind to determine if told the truth.

"Well, is he telling the truth or not?" Kofu appeared in front of his Royal Guards.

"Yes, my Lord!"

"Sorry for the inconvenience, my old friend, things around here have been out of the ordinary. So, I put the place on alert for any suspicious people or dark werewolves. Plus, the moon turning shades of red makes me worried. The last time I saw something like this was years ago during the Dark Wars. Is Samuel released from his prison that we trapped him into years ago?"

"Yes, Samuel is free, with the help from the Scarlet Witch, his grandson and unknowingly, my grandson Derrick."

"Whatever brought you here, my good friend must be important for you to be on my doorstep. What is wrong with the boy?"

"He's fallen under a spell. We need your help."

"With all this going on. I wish we would have had this little reunion under different circumstances."

"As you can see, my grandson Derrick was placed under a strong trance by Samuel." Sabrina took a deep breath. "Will you help us?"

"That shouldn't have been that hard to break with the likes of you two."

"We've tried, nothing is working. The spell is too strong."

Jarvis pulled Derrick off his shoulder and levitated him in a horizontal position.

Kofu examined him. The first thing he noticed was the golden compass hanging from Derrick's neck. "So, they finally gave it to him, huh? The last time I talked to King Damarco he wasn't thinking about giving Derrick a golden compass, but

I'm glad he did." Kofu checked Derrick's eyes and suspected the type of trance which affected him.

Beads of sweat dripped from Derrick's forehead, and his hands trembled.

Kofu noticed tattoos wrapping around Derrick's arms. "Bring him and follow me. I must confirm my suspicion."

Sabrina, Jarvis and Moon Slayer Twelve followed him as Derrick floated between them in transport.

Kofu stopped. "Royal Guards transform the wagon into a flower cart and lock the gates. Alert me immediately of any dark werewolves."

The group rushed to the third floor. "Jarvis lowered Derrick onto the table."

Out of nowhere, Kofu made his wizard book appear in front of him with a flick of a wrist. He proceeded to flip the pages using his mental power. "It's confirmed. Derrick is under a dream trance spell. Do you see these tattoos forming on his wrist?"

"What are they?" Jarvis bent to get a closer look at the tattoos.

"They're called the Rings of Amber. They're used to lock someone in a dream state of mind, forever."

"What!" Sabrina slammed her fist onto the table.

"If that line creates a full ring around his wrist, he will be gone forever; and whoever placed these on him wanted to use him as a weapon."

"What about the trance?"

"The Rings of Amber is a trance and locking spell. You would have to know what you're doing to perform this type of magic."

"How can we proceed without losing Derrick?" Sabrina sighed.

"I will have to send one of you into his dream to bring him back."

"I thought his gold compass protected him from spells." Jarvis frowned with worry.

"If it weren't for that dark magic that was already in his body, it would have stopped it. Someone has to enter his dream, and if you don't make it back before the Rings of Amber close, you will be trapped in Derrick's dreamworld." His eyes darted between Jarvis and Sabrina. "Now, who will go in his dream?"

"Me! I will go in." Sabrina looked at Jarvis.

"No, you're not healed yet; I will go."

"Remember Jarvis; you only have one hour from when you get in there to retrieve him. One more thing, your magic is of no use to you in there."

22. You Failed

Back at Waldorf Academy, Reign managed to escape from the rubble by using her magic and set out on a mission to find Derrick. That's when she saw Samuel and Barrett. *If I follow them, I'll find Derrick.*

They traveled through the academy down the back steps and proceeded through the forest. Once in the woods, Reign found it hard to keep up, due to the thick bushes, but eventually found her way to their location. She peered through the bushes staring at the Scarlet Witch fixing potions in some mini arena.

Samuel kissed the Scarlet Witch on her cheek while Barrett took a seat in the arena.

Reign turned back toward the Scarlet Witch, who flipped through the *Red Wizard Book*. "Samuel honey, you survived that little stunt that we did to you?"

"Oh, oh I did? I'm kind of surprised that my grandson grew a pair."

Barrett looked over at them with a grim look, then looked back toward the arena. "Enough with the small talk, can we get this party started or what?"

"What party are you talking about? The one where you tried to take my powers." Samuel glowered toward Barrett.

"No party, just a spell from the book that I'm doing on this subject, that's all." The Scarlet Witch cackled in delight.

"What subject?" Samuel sniffed the air.

"This one, bring him out." The Scarlet Witch darted her eyes toward Howling Fang.

"Lord Bloodstone, Sir! We've lost Derrick!" He held a tight leash around Silver's throat.

"Let me get this straight. You lost a person who was under a trance. He was standing before you. How hard is it to pick him up and bring him here?" Barrett stormed toward Howling Fang.

"Me and a few others were on our way to retrieve him for you when Sabrina took off with him, but we have his grandmother's dog."

"What did I tell you the last time if you screw up again?"

"You would kill me."

"Yeah, ha, ha, that's right? Why don't you stick around for a little bit? You might like the show. What direction was Sabrina heading?"

"Towards Copper Town."

Reign shocked to see Silver heaved a sigh of relief after she learned of Derrick's escape. *What is Silver doing here?*

She observed as the Scarlet Witch conjure up a spell from the *Red Wizard Book*. "Doggy-tails and eyes of newt turn this wolf into a fighting brute." A collar appeared in her hand. She placed a crystal in one of the loops and with a flick of her wrist; the collar appeared around Silver's neck.

Silver's whole demeanor changed, his fur changed to a reddish brown, and a strange aura radiated from him.

Reign didn't recognize Silver anymore. She slowly moved away from the area to search for Derrick.

"I think I'm going to rename him, Saber Wolf, he looks better now." Barrett beamed with pride. He turned back toward Howling Fang. "Now back to you, I'm tired of the stupidity I have around me! So, I think it's time to purge the flock."

He snapped his fingers, and the Howling Fang appeared in the arena. Barrett signaled to his new pet to attack.

Howling Fang tried to escape, but Samuel summoned up a dome surrounding the arena. The wounded werewolf searched for an exit but didn't find one. He growled, pumped his chest, extended his claws, and darted around Silver. Silver hit the ground with his paw. This made the ground shake and knocked over Howling Fang.

"They fight more like cats than beasts." Barrett pursed his lips.

Howling Fang stood and darted around Silver creating a gray fog blackening the area. Inside the gray fog, Howling Fang darted in and out of the fog swiping his sharp claws into Silver's flesh. After a minute, Silver got a hold on him, and then ripped him apart.

23. Fighting Demons

Back at Kofu's, Derrick lay lost in his dream controlled by the trance spell. Sabrina sighed. "Jarvis, please tell me you can do this. We can't lose him to Samuel or you to the Scarlet Witch."

"You're not telling me anything I don't already know."

Sabrina placed her palm onto Derrick's forehead. "I know he's in there. I can feel him dreaming."

Kofu cleared his throat. "Remember you will only have one hour."

***

Derrick woke up in front of the Royal Council. He immediately stood, dusted himself off and saluted them. Nervous and speechless, his stomach bubbled as he waited for someone to speak.

"Derrick, we are here to sentence you to death. The evidence is all here in front of me that shows the despicable and heinous crimes you've committed against your people." King Damarco spat into a cup. "You have disgraced your family and your kingdom."

"What crimes are you talking referring to? I shouldn't even be up here. You already sentenced me to banishment on Avalon Island."

"Silence! You disgust me."

"Wait, I'm your son; you're just going to discard me like that? I didn't do anything; someone is lying. Mom, you're just going to sit there and let them do this to me?"

Queen Gabriella's eyes lit with fire. "You're not a son of mine, not with all this evidence in front of me. We sentence you to death at high noon."

"Grandpa told me you wanted us to be a family and now you give me the death penalty? You've left me to be raise by

patrol members, who turned out to be more of a parent than both of you."

Two Royal Guards placed magical handcuffs onto Derrick's wrists and escorted him to his cell.

Right at that moment, Jarvis arrived into Derrick's mind outside of Sand Brook Wizard Academy. He approached the gates and suddenly stopped in his tracks.

"Halt! Announce who you are or die where you stand." The Royal Guard aimed his wand toward him.

"I'm Queen Gabriella's father; I'm here to see King Damarco and my daughter."

"They don't want to see you, old man. Now leave!"

Jarvis reached for his wand.

"You are a fool old man. Think before you do that, it will be your last."

"At least tell me where Derrick is?"

"He's in the cell waiting for his sentencing. Now leave!"

Jarvis backed away from the Royal Guard and proceeded into the forest thinking of a plan of action. He rustled a few weapons and rope from the nearby village and waited until dark to set his plan in motion.

Jarvis crept into the Academy ground. With a piece of the rope, he lassoed it to the end of his arrow; and then shot it toward a ledge where it landed underneath. He proceeded to scale the wall. Every time he saw a shadow of a Royal Guard who patrolled the area, he stopped climbing. Once he made it to the ledge, he used his bolas to tie up one of the Royal Guards and then knocked him out. He slid away into a dark corner and then waited for the other Royal Guard to pass. Once within reach, he slit his throat and pushed him over the ledge into the river below.

After Jarvis changed his clothes to the Royal Guard's, he proceeded through the Academy searching for Derrick. His mind played tricks on him, and he knew the longer he stayed in Derrick's mind with this parasite, the higher the risks increased. He had less than one hour, or he would be a slave to it and this place for eternity.

On the way to the cellblock to rescue his grandson, a high-ranking Royal Guard confronted Jarvis.

"What are you doing down here? You're supposed to be on the roof patrolling."

"I was until Royal Patrol Member Three ordered me to report to the cell for additional security." Jarvis averted his gaze avoiding eye contact with the high-ranking Royal Guard.

"Why would he step on my toes with my guard without speaking to me? Follow me; I don't like my authority overridden."

As Jarvis followed behind the high-ranking Royal Guard, he quickly defeated him with a hand-to-hand technique; and then he dragged him to a nearby room. He proceeded to the basement where he located his grandson who sat in his cell. An expression of defeat covered his face.

"Derrick, Derrick, it's me, Jarvis."

"What do you want?"

"I'm here to rescue you."

"What are you talking about? I deserve to be here for my crimes and sins."

"Derrick, this place is not real! A parasite is manipulating your memories." Jarvis could tell the parasite was almost in control of Derrick.

"My mom doesn't want me; nor my dad. I hurt people wherever I go. Maybe this is where I'm supposed to be, now leave me alone. Guards, Guards, intruder alert!"

Five guards rushed in, and a scuffle occurred tossing Jarvis into a cell next to his grandson.

"I guess now, we're here together, Grandson, but I'm not going to let you go down like this in this reality." Jarvis stood from his bench and gripped the bars; his demeanor intense. "Now, look at me, Derrick!"

Derrick glanced up at his granddad. "I'm cold, Grandpa, I don't have the motivation to escape this place."

"Derrick, lend me some of your power."

Derrick reached out transferring some of his mental power.

Jarvis received a vision which used it to show the true image of what was going on outside his grandson's brain. A flash of him as he followed Reign while she fled toward Copper Town, and then one of Sabrina struggling to hold Jarvis's mind clear from the parasite. "This is not the Derrick I know as my grandson. This is a Derrick who let a parasite control who he is and his reality. This is a Derrick who gave up on himself." Jarvis focused hard and created a new vision for Derrick to receive; a vision of confidence and strength.

As Derrick stood to his feet, the chains around his wrists and ankles fell to the ground. His depressed demeanor quickly changed to one of power. "I got this grandpa." He raised his arm, and the door of the cells opened.

The alert sounded, and all the Royal Guards rushed into the room.

"You won't get me this time." Derrick swirled his hands creating a windstorm and the Royal Guards bolted. As they reached the exit, Derrick threw an energy ball and knocked them out. "Okay, Grandpa, it's time you leave my mind. I'll join you on the other side as soon as I rid myself of this parasite. We have a war to be won."

***

Sabrina and Kofu watched over both Derrick and Jarvis waiting for them to return from the trance state.

Kofu scribed a message to King Damarco. "Please send reinforcements. We're under attack. I have Derrick. We must save the Prince." He tied the note to Emerald's leg, his pet hawk, and sent him on his journey.

Jarvis' eyes flickered, and then they blinked.

Sabrina hugged and kissed him. "Welcome back." She gazed at Derrick. "If you succeeded, he'd be awake. What went wrong?"

The tattoos around Derrick's wrists crept closer to merging to a complete circle.

Sabrina took a deep breath. "We don't have much time. Go back in there and retrieve my grandson."

"Wait, wait for it." Jarvis smiled. "Can I have some water please?"

"Water! Get back inside Derrick's mind."

"Look, Sabrina." Jarvis' eyes darted toward his grandson.

Derrick's eyes flickered as he turned his head. "Grandma, can I have some water?"

"Now you know why I asked for some." Jarvis winked at Sabrina.

Sabrina bolted over to her grandson and gave him a huge bear hug. After that, she flicked her wrist and made a cup of water appear in her hand. "I believe you asked for this." She handed the cup to Derrick.

"Where's Atlas? Has anybody found him yet?"

***

After an hour of flying, Reign landed in Cooper Town. A brown, black and white cat approached her flicking her tail. "I'm Kasha; Kofu sent me to retrieve you."

"Hi Kasha, have you seen Derrick?"

"I have. He's back at Kofu's place safe and sound, waiting for your arrival. Now enough with the short talk, we have to leave now."

"Get on my broom; we can get there faster."

"No, we must keep a low profile since you're still being followed. We have to lose whoever is following you."

Reign and Kasha ran through the cobbled streets of Copper Town. They jumped in and out of alleys and darted behind parked carriages and wagons. They managed to lose the person who followed them and made it safely to Kofu's place.

Kasha stopped in front of two buildings. "Reign, wait right there." She walked through a small vent in the saloon building.

Reign's brow creased. *I'm not going through that vent.* As Reign stood to wait for Kasha, a few folks exited the Saloon; smoke poured out the door. They waved at her. "Good morning young lady."

"And a good morning to you."

The people froze, and the two-building slid to either side revealing a gorgeous three-story building with Kasha waiting for her. "Step inside, Reign."

Once up the stairs, Reign entered the room scanning for Derrick. A white-toothed grin crossed her face the moment she spotted him. "Derrick! I'm so happy you're alive."

"That makes two of us."

She immediately sprinted to him and wrapped her arms around him.

***

Four hours later, Barrett's carriage with Samuel and the Scarlet Witch inside arrived in Copper Town stopping at the end of the bridge. An emergency alert alarm rang out throughout town.

Barrett cupped his hand behind his ear. "Hear that? Something is wrong."

His lackey ran up to his carriage. "Lord Bloodstone, we tried to follow Reign, but we lost her in town between Seventh Avenue and Sunset Street."

"It's fine; I'll unleash my new pet to find her and Derrick. Send in my Saber wolf; I don't want any mistakes this time."

"Right away, Lord Bloodstone."

"Scarlet Witch, I'll need you to place a dome over this town. We don't need any unwanted individuals interfering."

A few minutes later, General's reserves arrived and lined up in front of Barrett. Three steam-powered tanks and one hundred troops marched in stopping in front of him too. The General poked his head out of the middle tank. "You two strangers and your group are not welcome. As a resident and local law enforcement officer of this town, I order you and your group of delinquents to leave."

"Or else what?" Samuel snarled at the General.

"I will fire on you and destroy you and your men."

"Is this all the men you brought to defeat us? That's laughable."

The dark werewolves now halfway across the bridge charged toward the General.

The General raised his hand.

The first round of infantry fired their muskets at the dark werewolves. "Boom, Boom!" Several werewolves fell but got back up.

The General's face turned red. "Second infantry, Fire!" *Nothing is working*. "Attack!" He quickly dropped his hand, and the troops charged the dark werewolves.

The tanks fired small projectiles at them. After ten minutes, the battle ceased.

The General raised his hand. "Troops, retreat!"

***

Back at Kofu's place, everyone gathered around an oak table. Kofu flicked his wrist, and a map of Copper Town appeared onto the table. He pointed to their location from the bridges that surrounded the town. "We're here between Fifth Street and Maple Street. Barrett will be crossing Smoking River Bridge from the north. My sources informed me he has a large group of dark werewolves waiting for his signal to verge onto Copper Town using the other bridge. I am waiting for additional reinforcements from King Damarco, plus we have my army. We need to split up into two groups and defend Copper Town until they get here."

Sabrina nodded in affirmation. "We must retrieve the *Red Wizard Book* and figure out how to reverse the spell placed upon the Moon. We need a distraction."

"I got it, Grandpa; I need you to create a thick fog so it can block out the Moon to weaken Barrett and his dark werewolves. Kofu, I need your Warrior cats to retrieve the book." Derrick stood proud.

Reign tapped the table. "Sabrina, I hate to be the bearer of bad news, but Barrett captured Silver and cast a spell turning him into something evil."

"I will kill him for that." Sabrina clenched her fists; the floor quacked, and items fell from the shelves.

A Royal Guard entered the room. "My Lord, dark werewolves are heading this way with the help of some reddish wolf. You must leave now! Also, there is a dome forming around the town."

Kofu licked his lips. "Everyone has their assignments. Does anyone have any questions before we engage in battle?" He made eye contact with everyone in the room. "Very well, disperse and defend. Good luck to you all."

Kofu strode over to a closed door and turned the knob; his power changed the room next door.

The dark werewolves breached the barrier and made their way into Kofu's place. Moon Slayer Twelve stayed to block their escape. The group rushed into the room which led to an empty barber shop two streets over. The door slammed shut.

Outside the palace, Kofu, Jarvis, Sabrina, Derrick, Kasha, and Reign gazed at the dome.

Jarvis pursed his lips. "We need to take down whoever is forming that dome. Otherwise, the reinforcements won't get through."

Sabrina nodded. "I'll handle it. I'll need Reign and Kasha to back me up."

"Count us in." Reign gazed toward Kasha.

"I'm definitely in."

"This way girls." The three vacated the area toward their mission.

Dark werewolves scattered throughout the town and caused mayhem wherever they went.

Hiding in the barber's shop, Derrick noticed Barrett's carriage heading down the street. "I've got you this time." He focused his mental power and hurled an energy ball toward it ripping it half. Derrick approached the carriage and peeped inside. "Where are they? Grandpa, they're not here."

"I thought if we ride around, you might show up. My Granddad thought I was crazy." Barrett appeared from around the corner.

"Oh Barrett, this time, I will end this." Derrick seethed in anger.

Samuel emerged from the shadows to face Kofu. "Hi Kofu, my old friend, you thought you wouldn't see me again, didn't you? After all, you and the Royal Council banished me to the dark void."

"I had a feeling that I would see your no- talent, spoiled, egomaniacal self again."

Derrick lunged toward Barrett who held up his palm sending a red energy bolt and immediately knocked him back into a parked carriage.

Jarvis rushed over to help him.

"No Grandpa, I've got this battle."

"Are you sure?"

Derrick nodded.

"Remain calm down and focus on the task at hand."

"Like I won't."

Barrett signaled his dark werewolves to attack as Kofu called for his warrior cats, who appeared out of alleys and transformed into their human-like form with weapons.

Jarvis created a thick fog to block out the Moon to make it an even fight.

24. Conquering Your Fears

The reinforcements from King Damarco trapped outside the dome stood helpless.

Kasha, Sabrina, and Reign made their way toward the dome wall toward the south. "Sabrina and Reign, I sense something evil tracking us." She immediately came to a halt.

Before them stood the Scarlet Witch in the middle of a market square surrounded by dark werewolves who patrolled the area.

Sabrina took a deep breath. "Reign, you and I will take on the Scarlet Witch. Kasha, you handle the werewolves."

Once Kasha stepped out into the opening, she flicked her tail. "Oh, dark werewolves, catch me if you can."

The werewolves charged her as she led them in a chase down a back alley.

Sabrina and Reign armed up and attacked the Scarlet Witch from both sides, but as they got closer, Saber now under her control came from the fire escapes of a building. He landed on a parked steam-powered car and then lunged toward Reign who saw his shadow and quickly defended herself with her bow. She struggled to get Saber off her. His massive weight dented her bow.

Sabrina bolted toward the Scarlet Witch who stopped her in her footsteps with a flick of her wrist and froze her in her steps.

***

The dark werewolves closed in on Kasha's heels. She ran into an alley, and to her relief, several warrior cats emerged from the trash can, side streets, and fire escapes.

"Am I glad to see you."

The warrior cats threw magical nets over two of the dark werewolves while the other two surrounded by twelve cats with steel spears fought. They scrapped for twenty minutes until no more dark werewolves remained.

Kasha took a deep breath. "Warrior cats, thank you again. I still need your help."

"We'll follow you."

Reign's bow broke as she reached for her knife. She stabbed Saber in the abdomen. He released Reign as he jumped back, then reached down and pulled out the knife with his mouth.

***

Sabrina struggled to free herself from the Scarlet Witch's spell. *Will I survive this? Usually Silver helps me in situations like this one.* Sabrina's arms started moving with both knives aimed towards her throat, and then stopped against her throat. She glared at the Scarlet Witch, who was attacked by the warrior cats now, then back at Reign who was still going toe to toe with Silver. Reign stood up and then reached for her wand. Saber shook his fur creating a fiery aura around him. She used her power to toss a parked wagon which sat to the left of her at Saber, which he quickly leaped over and continued toward her then she sent a metal armor carriage crashing hard into him knocking Saber out cold.

While the warrior cats distracted, the Scarlet Witch lost control of Sabrina. This allowed Sabrina to have control of her body. She waited for an opening to strike the Scarlet Witch with her knife. As the Scarlet Witch swung at one of the warrior cats, Sabrina quickly hit her in the back. The Scarlet Witch screamed in pain, then called for more backup from her dark werewolves and then, disappeared into the shadow.

The dome started to retract, and that put a smile on Sabrina's face, but she still wondered how Jarvis and Derrick were handling their situation. She looked over at Reign, who had Saber tied down, thanks for the help of the warrior cats, but when she tried to pull the collar out of Saber's neck, his power knocked them back, and then he escaped.

Once the dome came down, the reserves from King Damarco immediately surged on the dark werewolves.

Barrett gasped as he leaned forward. *Why don't I feel as strong? We're losing the fight.* He happened to glance toward the Moon covered by a thick fog. He parted the thick fog and bathed in the red moonlight as his strength and size increased. He transformed back into a dark werewolf.

Samuel used his power to lift the water surrounding the town and used it to wipe out the battlefield.

Derrick, Jarvis, and Kofu blocked the avalanche of water; each held palms toward the water wall and pushed it back with their collective energy.

Barrett, with three dark werewolves, survived and continued to attack Derrick and Jarvis, while Kofu took on Samuel.

Derrick had a tough time keeping up with Barrett's speed. The onslaught attack of Barrett's blows to Derrick's face and stomach felt like his bones shattered. Barrett dragged Derrick all over the streets of Copper Town until he let Derrick's body roll into a nearby building. Derrick's compass glowed intensely as he tried to stand to wipe the blood from his mouth. A white cloud formed around Derrick which healed him. Derrick's pupil's turned golden, and then gloves covered his hands. He trembled as he received a surge of energy as a golden trench coat covered him as if to shield him. After nodding, a golden hue surrounded him which upgraded his wand to gold that appeared in his hand.

Barrett glowered toward Derrick. "I'm going to finish you once and for all." As he charged Derrick, Barrett's claws enlarged like spears for a final strike to kill Derrick. Barrett penetrated the cloud but stopped immediately; his whole body lifted, and then hurled to the ground. Barrett stood and shot an energy blast at Derrick knocking him back.

Derrick regrouped.

Barrett transported behind him placing Derrick in a full nelson. Derrick struggled to wiggle from the grasp before he slammed the back of his head into Barrett's snout, and then tossed him to the ground. Derrick pointed his wand toward Barrett. "A chain, a chain, is what you need, I never again want to see thee."

The golden compass glowed brighter as Barrett grew smaller and smaller until he fit inside his magic notebook to be trapped forever.

Derrick smiled. "Grandma, I'm glad you taught me that locking spell."

On the other side, Jarvis had his hands full surrounded by three dark werewolves. He reached for his notebook, drew two likenesses of himself, crumbled up the paper into a ball, and then lit them on fire. "Double of thy, make two stone likeness of me."

The Jarvis clones entered the battle area carrying a mix of paper and stone. They fought along at Jarvis' side. One killed a dark werewolf by slicing off his head with his sword and the other attacked with his strength. Eventually, the three killed the dark werewolves.

After witnessing his grandson sealed into Derrick's notebook, Samuel's blood boiled. He flipped through the pages of the *Red Wizard Book* for an evolving spell. Samuel ripped his trench coat as the wind increased; gradually he transformed into a dark werewolf with burgundy and gray fur. Samuel's head and face converted back to normal, but his body kept the form of the dark werewolf. He looked menacing and gave off intense energy.

Jarvis knew that he would need both Kofu and Derrick to defeat Samuel new form. Kofu went head to head in a fight with Samuel who now tossed him as if a sack full of rice. With the help of Kofu's warrior cats, Samuel managed to lose his grip of the *Red Wizard Book*.

Jarvis transported to his grandson. "Derrick, you must distract Samuel. I'm going to summon the Dark Void."

"You can count on me, Grandpa." Derrick targeted his energy toward Samuel. "Darkness of Moon I need a lock, lock the evil Samuel in an ice block."

The locking spell held Samuel for several minutes before he broke free shattering the ice block. Samuel and Derrick fought for some time blocking and countering each other's attack until the Dark Void opened.

Derrick's eyes glowed as his compass did too. "Dark of Moon, I need your strength to lock this man in an iced link. One entombed in the block, I command you never to unlock." *This better work.*

The ground rumbled opening the Dark Void, and the temperature dropped. A block of ice surrounded Samuel.

Derrick's fist pumped into the air. "We did it. Everyone we did it."

"Not so fast, grandson. Everyone, use your magic powers and push Samuel into the Dark Void."

Jarvis, Kofu, Derrick, and Sabrina focused their powers as Samuel slipped into the Dark Void. In an instant, the Dark Void closed.

They all took a deep breath.

Derrick smiled. "Now, now we have done it. Has anybody located Atlas?" His heart sank.

Sabrina raised her palms toward the dark red moon. "Man, on the Moon come back to me, let us again set you free." The red moon soon glowed white.

The wind increased as Derrick's golden gloves, gold trench coat and wand converted back into their original form. "Darn, I really was hoping I could keep those."

Kofu stepped forward. "Thank you all for the help. Copper Town was destroyed, but if we all use our magic, we can fix the fallen buildings and make our town beautiful again. Then we'll celebrate with a fine meal and drink."

With a zip and a zap, the rubble turned to the beautiful city.

***

Kofu's palace hall filled with merriment as they gathered to celebrate. Musician's played as people danced. Plenty of food and drink for all.

Sabrina danced with Jarvis. "Tonight's a fine celebration for life."

"I agree."

"Look at Derrick dancing with Reign. I think he's got a crush on her."

"She's a good warrior."

Derrick led Reign off the dance floor. "Let's go to the roof and Moon watch."

"Why Derrick, I thought you'd never ask." She blushed and giggled as he led her toward the exit.

When they reached the flat roof, Derrick waved his wand, and a blanket appeared on the ground. "My lady, please have a seat." They eased onto the blanket and then leaned with their backs against the rock wall. They stared at the Moon.

Derrick sighed as he frowned. "I'm glad the mayhem is over, but I don't know what I'm going to say to the King and Queen when I return to face them."

"My Prince, you mean your parents, don't you?"

"I guess so; I'm trying to wrap my head around all of this. I don't know where to start. I have so much on my mind that I want to say to the King and Queen and I'm confused and worried because I haven't seen my mom since she left with the Moon Slayers and my dad helping the Royal Patrol Meds. I thought they both would be here tonight."

"Try not to worry about that. Your dad is probably up to his neck treating people, and your mom is a strong warrior."

"I still don't know where to begin with the King and Queen."

"Start with one question and work from there; don't worry, I got your back if you need me, Derrick." A meteor dashed across the twinkling starry sky. "Did you see that?"

"I sure did. It's a great night for star gazing."

"The Moon looks beautiful tonight too, doesn't it?" Reign sighed as her eyes twinkled like diamonds.

"Yeah, it sure does! You look beautiful tonight as well."

Reign's cheeks blushed.

He gently guided her face toward his. They stared into each other's eyes, and then slowly passionately kissed.

Derrick grinned larger than life. "That kiss was way much better than the one we shared in my dream trance."

To be continued.

ABOUT THE AUTHOR

Robert Herring Jr resides in Pittsburgh, PA. He has authored short stories since high school. His first story was about a crazy day with his family. Robert Herring always wanted to author a novel, so he sat down one day started, and in 2016 he accomplished his dream. He earned his Associate degree in Computer Drafting and Design from ITT Technical Institute.

Thank you for reading my novel. I hope you enjoyed it. If you will, please leave an honest review on Amazon or Goodreads and www.robertbherringjr.com Be on the lookout for new books from me.

56851354R10096

Made in the USA
Middletown, DE
26 July 2019